THE MARKET ON BLUEBERRY BAY

BLUEBERRY BAY

ELLEN JOY

To my readers. You give me more inspiration than you know.

Click HERE or visit ellenjoyauthor.com for more information about all of Ellen's books.

The Lighthouse on Blueberry Bay
The Fabric Shop on Blueberry Bay

Beach Rose Secrets

CHAPTER 1

*R*emy didn't know what to think about her father and Ginny, but as she stared out the window at the blueberry fields where Gordon and Ginny talked, she was certain something was happening between the two of them.

"Do you think they're like..." she began to say to her sister, Meredith, who sat at the counter sipping her morning coffee.

"Like...?" Meredith said, continuing to carry out the word until Remy finished her sentence.

"Into each other?" Remy asked, grimacing at the idea of her seventy-five-year-old father being into someone other than her mother.

Meredith sipped her coffee, barely hiding her smirk. "I think it's cute."

Remy didn't.

"I think Ginny's sweet and all, but the two of them together?" Remy wasn't sure why it felt stranger than she had anticipated. She couldn't expect her father to never date again. Her mother had passed away over two years ago. Gordon deserved a little bit of happiness in his life.

But love wasn't the only way to be happy. Sometimes people

just needed to learn to love life by themselves. Not depend on others to create their happiness.

Remy had certainly learned that the hard way.

"Why do you have a problem with it?" Meredith asked, looking out at the couple in the fields.

"I don't have a *problem* with it. It's just that..." Remy sighed. "I just want him to be happy."

"He seems to be happy." Meredith gestured her chin at the two standing in the middle of the field giggling together. "He looks like a little kid laughing."

Remy looked at her father. Gordon did look happy. So did Ginny. And Remy adored Ginny. The neighbor next door to her sister's cottage had been nothing but generous and helpful to the sisters when they had first arrived in Maine. Not to mention all the other things over the years Ginny had done behind the scenes to help their family.

She should be happy her father was happy.

But...she wasn't. Something about it made her anxious.

"Good morning," a male voice said from the back porch.

Quinn Michaud, her sister's boyfriend and Ginny's son, walked into the house from the screened porch and straight to Meredith. He gave a small wave to Remy, but his attention and stride were focused on Meredith, who sat grinning at him. They kissed right away, a tender, warm kiss that made Remy look away and back to Gordon and Ginny.

Two Gs, she thought to herself. "Not too many people with a name that starts with G."

She looked back at Meredith and Quinn, expecting them to be a part of her random thought, but they were lost in their own conversation.

"What did you say?" Meredith asked, clearly not listening to Remy.

Remy looked back at the fields, shaking her head. "It's nothing."

"We're going to the hardware store soon, if you want to come with us," Meredith said to Remy. Meredith's newest project was winterizing the cottage after a harsh winter—new windows, new insulation in the attic and the basement. During the winter, the upstairs barely had heat. When the previous owner, Jacob, lived there, he slept downstairs next to the woodstove on really cold nights.

The project would be a big one. Meredith would be doing more than just fixing up the place; she would be putting real money into renovating it for her wants and needs. Taking on this project meant Meredith would be staying at the cottage indefinitely.

Remy, on the other hand, was homeless.

"No, I'm good, thanks," Remy said, not knowing what her plan for the day would be.

She had nothing to do and nowhere to go.

She couldn't go back to Joe, not with what had happened after the festival.

Not that she wanted to go back.

She'd had legal documents drawn up to start their separation. She had taken one weekend to go through all their things and took only what she needed. She wanted nothing to do with Joe's money, Joe's houses, or Joe's businesses. The prenup certainly made it clear—being his wife had no effect on his business.

Fifteen years seemed to have no effect on Joe, either. After he'd left that weekend of the festival, he hadn't spoken to her again. Not even when they met face-to-face with their attorneys.

Remy stepped out to the back porch, wishing last summer hadn't ended so quickly. Back in Massachusetts, spring had already come and gone, yet up here in Maine, the leaves hadn't even budded. She'd love to jump in the water and go for a morning swim, but the temperatures still held the winter chill, and she needed a coat to sit outside that morning.

What would she do with her life?

"I think I'll go to the market and grab some stuff," she said, thinking about dinner. "I feel like fish tonight."

"Oh, well, Quinn and I were planning on having dinner..." Meredith looked at Quinn, having that silent conversation that couples have with each other.

"You should come with us," Quinn quickly said, catching on.

Remy wished so badly she could be happy for her sister and not be annoyed. "I'm fine, you guys. You don't have to invite me to dinner."

Quinn and Meredith looked at each other.

Remy rolled her eyes. "I'm fine." She grabbed her cup of coffee and put her winter coat on. "I'm going to have my coffee on the porch."

She took her phone and opened the back door, then sat down on the daybed and pulled up the blankets she had put out there.

What was she going to do? The question kept crashing into her head like the waves against the granite shores of Blueberry Bay, pounding over and over again.

She had no income other than Joe's alimony, which hadn't begun. Her interior design gigs had dried up. She couldn't even call it a business when her clients were her friends. She didn't have a business card, or a website, or an employee, other than her mom helping. But now, she didn't even have her mom. She didn't have anything.

Except her family. She had her family, and that was enough for her right now.

Meredith had been so helpful through everything. She couldn't have asked for a better sister. Both she and Gordon had been her support throughout this whole situation with Joe.

She was blessed.

Which was why Remy needed to figure out her plans so she wasn't living off her sister's generosity too long.

She stared out from her sister's cottage, which sat on the coast of Maine along the mighty Atlantic, feeling so small in that moment. That morning, the waves crashed into the granite cliffs, remnants of a late winter storm from the night before. If one of those waves were to sweep her up and take her out to sea, she'd leave nothing behind. What had she contributed to this world?

She was a too-busy daughter, a half there sister, and somebody's ex-wife.

She probably wouldn't even make it into Joe's obituary.

She was a forty-five-year-old spinster who didn't even have a cat.

The spray from a wave suspended in the air for a split second before falling back down and splattering against the rock cliffs.

She didn't want to leave her sister's seaside cottage, named perfectly as The Cottage by the Sea, but how long was she going to live off everyone else in her life?

She looked at the pale blue sky. She had to figure things out before she became a burden.

Through the kitchen window, Meredith and Quinn sat happily together at the counter, hand in hand, sipping coffee. She may not be a burden at this point, but she would be soon.

Even Gordon seemed to be moving on and finding his own happiness.

She downed her coffee, got up from her spot on the porch, and headed inside.

"I think I'm going to run to town," she said, passing quickly through the kitchen. "I'm going to buy some fish for tonight. Will Kyle and Ginny be around tonight?"

"I think Kyle has a team dinner," Meredith said. "And Gordon and Ginny are going to the VFW's spaghetti dinner."

"Are you sure you don't want to join us?" Quinn said. "We're headed to The Farmhouse."

Remy hadn't eaten at the rustic renovated barn that deserved a five-star review for its romantic atmosphere alone.

"Thanks, but I'm good." Remy couldn't believe this was her life.

A year ago, she had so many invitations and benefits and different events lined up that she'd had no free time.

Now, she would be dining alone.

But she didn't need others around. She could be by herself. She wasn't falling apart because her husband didn't love her anymore.

She just needed to figure things out.

"Well, I'm headed out," she said, not giving specifics because she didn't really have any. She just knew she couldn't stay in the house with all the happy couples. Even Kyle and his girlfriend were constantly showing affection.

But what could she do for a job?

She could paint using her useless art degree from a state school in Massachusetts. Not like her mother's art education in Paris or Meredith's father's talent for evoking emotions of the viewers. She had basic skills. If that.

She could paint houses, and walls, and choose colors. She had a knack at design, but not a degree, and no accolades or true recommendations.

Just friends of friends.

Even her close friend Greg hadn't been able to find her a job in Boston. He had been her best bet.

She grabbed her phone and purse and left. She looked out at the blueberry fields, where Ginny and Gordon were standing, and waved. They didn't even notice her.

She scanned for Quinn's son's truck but realized Kyle was in school.

She got into her car and sat, letting it heat up before pulling out of the driveway. She had no destination now that she didn't need to make dinner. She didn't have anywhere to go.

She pulled out, following the road to town. She decided to go to the market anyway and maybe stop at the park and see her mother. Well, her mother's statue.

She took a right onto Main Street, driving the winding road to the little town of Blueberry Bay. The closer she got to town, the more houses lined the street, mostly New England style capes and colonials, all built centuries ago with some of the same family names still inside. Most were painted white or were gray clapboard shingles. All were a bit worn down by the weather.

Unlike other New England seaside towns, where only the wealthy had the privileges of the shore, most of the houses along the harbor's edge were local fisherman and townies. There were some summer homes and pricey estates along the coast, but not like along Massachusetts' coasts or even southern Maine. Way up here, in what the locals referred to as Down East, everyone got to enjoy the beauty of the Atlantic waters and live off it as well. Most of the town fished for lobsters—the rest survived on tourism.

When she pulled into her usual parking spot, she looked down at her phone. No calls. No friends checking in. No clients wanting her work. No one needing her expert advice.

She wondered, if she hadn't forced Meredith to let her come up to Maine that summer, if she had gone missing, would anyone have noticed?

Definitely not her husband.

Well, ex-husband.

Remy Moretti, ex-wife of Joseph Moretti, financial advisor and CEO of Moretti Investments.

She took off her seatbelt and considered how long she could afford to keep her luxury car in Maine. She couldn't even afford the premium gas to fill up the tank. She didn't even want to think about the oil changes. The German sedan proved useless in the winter months.

She looked out at the quaint little market that had become her favorite spot in Blueberry Bay. The local market surprisingly carried every kind of fish one could find in the waters of the Atlantic Ocean. The red exterior clapboard looked as though it had been on the building since its established date of 1843.

Just as she got out of the car, a loud horn blasted from behind her, making her jump.

"What the heck?" Remy swung around to see a truck stopped behind hers.

"You can't park there!" a man yelled from the driver's seat; his window open. His Maine accent was thick. "Pull your car out."

"Are you serious?" She looked at the parking spot. "I was here first."

She always parked up front.

"That's not a parking spot!" The man flung his hand around.

Remy shut her door and ignored him. The bearded flannel-wearing maniac reminded her more of someone from Boston than the overly friendly Maine residents.

"You've got to be kidding me, lady!" he yelled out. Then he threw the truck into drive and slammed the gas, screeching his wheels as he pulled behind the market.

Remy didn't know who that man was, but she was glad he took off.

"People are crazy," she muttered as she walked inside the market.

"Good morning," the owner, Emil, said to Remy.

"Hello, Mr. St. Germain," Remy greeted him as she stepped further inside. Immediately, the smells of ocean mixed with rustic wood. The sunlight streamed through the second story antique windows from the loft above. Muffled murmurs of customers talking echoed throughout the space.

"What can I get you today?" the older man asked.

"What do you suggest?" Remy smiled at the owner, leaving the decision fully in his hands.

"My son just pulled up," Emil said, jabbing his thumb behind him. "Why don't we look at the catch."

She turned in the direction of his thumb, when the big, burly truck driver stepped into the market. She hadn't noticed how attractive the man was while he was yelling through his truck window, but the whole tall, dark, and flannel really worked for him.

"That's your son?" She frowned as the bearded lumberjack came over to Emil and mumbled something. Remy swore he growled when he looked in her direction.

"Colby!" Emil said in a loud, booming voice. "Meet my favorite customer."

"I have." He placed his hands on his waist, avoiding the handshake she attempted to give to be polite. "Everything's out back. I wasn't able to unload."

He stared at her, shooting daggers through his intense, icy blue eyes.

"Yes, well, I can take something that's in your display already." She picked up a bottle of wine on a rack next to her instead of hissing back at the man named Colby. "No need to go in the back for me."

He didn't say anything, just stared at her, like a pit bull.

She walked down the glass cases and looked for something quickly, feeling pressured by Colby's presence.

"I've got some live oysters that would go great with the wine." Emil nodded at the bottle in her hands. "Some cod or Atlantic salmon would also pair nicely?"

With this, she noticed Colby roll his eyes as he grabbed a notebook and started writing something down.

Grumpy guy, she thought to herself. "You know what? I'll take the cod."

"Good choice!" Emil said in delight.

The market owner had become one of Remy's only friends in Blueberry Bay. Not that he was her actual friend, but she enjoyed their conversations and looked forward to hearing his suggestions and recommendations. Emil knew a lot about fish and cooking it. He also loved to tell a story, and Remy had learned a lot about the little town she was staying in through Emil.

"How much would you like today?" he asked.

"Um…" Remy paused, looking up from the case. Both men were waiting for her to answer. She felt pathetic ordering one serving, though if she got any more she would have to freeze what she didn't eat, which would almost be sacrilegious considering what a beautiful piece of fish it was. But she couldn't let this macho man know that she was eating alone. "I'll take enough for three."

"How's the house coming?" Emil asked. He turned to his son and said, "Remy is Jacob O'Neill's daughter."

"That's my sister, actually," she said, raising her finger at the faux pas. But she wasn't sure how to correct without going into extraneous detail. "Meredith Johnson. She's Jacob's daughter."

By the way Colby raised his eyebrows, wrinkling his forehead the way he did, it seemed that they didn't understand that Jacob was her sister's father, not hers.

"Right, sorry about that," Emil said. He held up a beautiful green acorn squash, big enough for a family. "This would be perfect with a bit of nutmeg and butter?" Emil was always right.

"It would." She took it out of his hands, along with the wrapped-up piece of fish.

"I think that'll do it for today," she said, when she noticed a sign up at the counter.

Help wanted.

She pulled out her wallet, wondering when Joe would cut off her credit cards. The judge hadn't finalized the divorce, but even her lawyers seemed pessimistic about the iron-clad prenup. She would get basic living expenses for a year.

The card beeped.

She looked up at the machine.

Card declined.

Her face immediately flushed with heat. "I'm so sorry. I…" She pulled out her debit card, hoping and praying Joe hadn't cut her off from their bank account. Could he do that? "Try this."

She slid the card through the machine, her cheeks burning, but it beeped back at her after she put in her pin.

So, Joe did follow through with his threats. He had completely cut her off.

"I am so sorry," she said, looking in her wallet. She had at least a hundred in cash. Thank goodness she had stopped the other day. Not too many people even took credit in Blueberry Bay. She looked at the last of her cash. Should she bury her pride and keep the money she had left? At least put away the forty-dollar bottle of wine? But with the way the smirk lingered on Colby's mouth as she fumbled through her purse, she did something only Mrs. Joe Moretti could do. "You can keep the change."

She threw the twenties down on the counter, grabbed her hundred-dollar meal for one and walked out.

CHAPTER 2

*R*emy got into her car and let out a long exhale. She picked up her phone and dialed Joe's direct line, but her number had been blocked.

She squeezed her fist, calling a number that would likely answer but would also charge her—her lawyer.

"Remy!" her attorney said into the phone. She had hired an up-and-coming female lawyer that hadn't been on retainer with Joe. "How can I help you?"

Remy was her biggest client.

"He cut off my credit and my debit," Remy said. "I thought he couldn't do that."

"He can…" her attorney said slowly.

"You're kidding me."

"You need to open your own banking and credit line so you can receive his alimony, which you can then use for living expenses, etc." Her voice sounded too young to be that of a very expensive attorney.

"But I have nothing set up," Remy said, flabbergasted at the lack of sympathy she was receiving from everyone—Joe, her attorney, the guy in the truck. "How can he just cut me off if the divorce hasn't even been finalized?"

"He can put a hold on all expenses."

"Like food?" Remy couldn't believe this. "He has money every-where and can get his hands on it whenever he wants. That's just not right to cut his wife off."

"You left the domain."

"Because I had to according to the prenup!" she screamed out.

"Well, the one thing you could have done is stay in the house until you found a new location."

"Will he feed me if I go back?" she asked sarcastically, but she might think about it if that's what it came down to. "I need some sort of cash, now."

"I can get you some cash until you set up a bank account and so forth."

Remy hadn't set anything up because she had wanted to wait until the divorce was finalized to change her name, and then she could set up an account under her original maiden name, Johnson.

"I'll go to the bank today," Remy said. "I'll let you know what happens."

Would a bank even let her open a checking account with no money?

She would have to talk to Gordon. Her father would know what to do. She didn't want to have to borrow money, but what would she do in the meantime?

How did she go from being in the upper class to suddenly broke?

Leaving Joe Moretti. That's how.

What did women do with no one to help them if they left their husband?

Remy supposed they had jobs.

They didn't believe their husbands when they said they would take care of them.

They learned to take care of themselves.

That was Remy's problem. She had believed Joe when he'd said he'd take care of her. She'd believed Joe when he told her she could have a choice in their life without working. She knew better. Her mother had warned her!

"Don't depend on your husband to be who you are," Jacqueline had said to her before the wedding. "You can still work and be a wife."

But Joe had insisted she quit working. "He wants me to be able to travel with him."

Remy's dream life had sat at her fingertips. She wasn't going to miss it to work as some assistant to a curator in a small museum no one ever visited when she could be flying to Dubai.

But the traveling, the vacations, the time Joe promised to spend with her, had all faded soon after the wedding. Then years of being Joe Moretti's wife had become her job. And it was the loneliest job she'd ever had. She'd run the houses, the staff, the events, and *everything* Joe needed. If she'd had a true title, it would not have been Joe's wife, but his executive assistant.

Who apparently didn't get paid.

As she checked her rearview mirror to reverse, she noticed her hands shaking. What was she going to do? She didn't want to live like this.

She pounded the steering wheel with her hands and screamed.

That's when she noticed the truck revving next to her. Was that man seriously waiting for her to leave?

Why did men think they owned everything?

"Give me a minute!" she yelled out in her car, not caring if the man in the truck could hear her or not. He was ridiculous. If she wasn't about to burst into tears, she might have turned off her car and got out again.

But instead, she shifted into reverse, whipped out of the parking spot, and threw it into drive, when out of the corner of her eye, she saw a No Parking sign.

Why hadn't she ever seen the sign before?

She tried to avoid the glare from the man in the truck as she pulled forward and away from the market, but that just made her tear up, making the road blurry. She pulled into another parking spot along the garden, put the car into park, and cried.

Sobbed, to be exact. A deep, wrenching sound reverberated out of her chest.

How could he leave her with nothing, knowing she had nothing?

Because he wanted her to suffer.

Remy looked out at the town garden. The sun shone off the bits of frost still remaining on the grass tips. The ocean looked even colder than usual. Her eyes went straight to the bronze mermaid statue. Like the sea smoke rising from the water, the sun's warmth steamed the frost on the statue, and it rose from the surface, almost making the whole thing lifelike.

She wished her mother would come out of the bronze like the frost steam and help her. She had never needed her mother more than right at that moment, and all she had was a frozen statue of her mother's upper body.

She hated that statue. Romantic, yes. But also tragic, hard, sad, and painful. All made by a guy she'd never met and hadn't been related to. When she blew her nose, she looked in the rearview to see truck guy staring at her from his perch in the truck. Then, to her horror, she saw him get out of his truck and start walking toward her car. She wasn't going to stick around to hear what he had to say. He probably wanted to point out the sign.

She turned the ignition and quickly pulled out of the parking spot, then took off just before he started to walk across the street. As she took a right, she noticed him stop and watch her drive away from the middle of the road.

Blueberry Bay was a small town, but she hoped to never see Emil's son again.

When she got home, she put away her dinner and sat in the living room, staring at one of her mother's paintings. Remy guessed it had been one of her first paintings she had done while married to Jacob, her first husband. Her mother had been a talented and successful artist. Remy had been gifted in the same ways, and in others, cursed. Remy could see beauty, knew how to put it together and space it apart, but she never knew how to create it. And Remy wanted so badly to create her own like her mother.

Jacqueline came into painting because of Jacob. She had never experimented or taken classes other than watercolor before she'd met him. The posh summer girl from Boston had found her medium by falling in love with a man who had given her everything she needed.

Joe wanted his wife to be his accessory. The person by his side. So, Remy had used her talents and love of art to dress impeccably, design their houses perfectly, and find beauty with the things around them like their art, food, and architecture. She had scoured every corner of the earth to find the right pieces for Joe's world, which she'd thought she was helping create for both of them.

The irony was that Joe had been her best client.

"Hey, baby girl," Gordon said as he came into the house.

She could feel the cold coming off him. Even in April, the weather held a bite to it.

"How are the blueberries?" she asked, ignoring the fact that Gordon had come from Ginny's house and not the blueberry fields.

"The frost didn't do any damage," he said, putting his coat and gloves into the closet by the front door. "I saw you got groceries. I just wanted to let you know that I'm going to—"

"I know, the spaghetti dinner," she said. "I got dinner for me."

He nodded. "You could join us."

She smiled but shook her head, hoping he wouldn't notice that she had been crying. "I have a very good meal planned with my favorite movie."

"Ah, *Mary Poppins*?" Gordon asked.

Remy couldn't even remember a time she had watched *Mary Poppins*.

"Isn't that your favorite movie?" she asked.

"No, it's your mother's!" he said, surprised she didn't know that. "She would beg you girls to watch it every time you had a movie night."

This made Gordon laugh, but Remy teared up.

"What's the matter?" Gordon asked, suddenly noticing her puffy eyes.

She shook her head, letting out a laugh, but it only came out like a sob. "I'm fine."

"What's wrong?" Gordon asked, now fully aware something was wrong.

She grabbed a tissue from its container on the side table. "He cut me off from the finances."

Gordon's face dropped into a seriousness she didn't see very frequently. "Did you call your lawyer?"

She sniffled and nodded. "I talked to her this morning when I left the market. When I realized my cards didn't work."

Gordon's eyes flickered with understanding.

Remy thought back to the truck guy's face when she had paid, which made her cry even more.

"It's time you get a better attorney," Gordon said. "Get this worked out right away."

"She's the best I can afford," Remy said, and Alicia Sommers had come highly recommended. "I can't change the fact that I signed the prenup."

"Prenup or not, that man is purposefully punishing you for leaving him." Gordon nailed it on the head. "He can't get away with that kind of behavior."

"Technically, he can," she said before blowing her nose. "He can remove me from all his assets and then give me my *deserved* amount, as determined by a judge. I need to have a bank account set up in order to do that, but I don't have a name or an address!"

Remy burst into tears—hard, frantic sobs—and she couldn't contain her sounds. Like a ravaged animal fighting for its last breath, she heaved in breaths, but her lungs constricted, tightening her rib cage like a noose.

"I have nothing to my name," she cried out. "And I don't even have a name."

Gordon's lips pursed together. "You don't need to worry about anything."

"I can't have my retired father paying for me." No, she couldn't have another man paying for her life. She knew what she needed to do. "I need to get a job," she said through a hiccupped breath. "But I don't even have references."

This brought more tears.

"We're going to the bank right now." Gordon stood up from the couch. "We're going to open up a checking account and get you what's rightfully owed to you after dealing with that narcissist for all those years."

Remy's chin quivered at this. She loved her father, but she really didn't want another man to solve her problems. She got into this mess because she hadn't done anything for herself. She needed to start learning how to live on her own.

Her mother had left a horrible situation with a small child and had done it on her own.

"I can do this on my own," she said.

"You think you'd let me suffer if the tables were turned?" Gordon said. "Let me help you."

"No." She sniffled some more. "This is something I need to do. Something I have to do."

She couldn't rely on everyone to get through this. She needed to learn to stand on her own two feet.

"I'll figure things out," she said. "Please, just let me figure things out."

CHAPTER 3

*R*emy didn't figure things out. Gordon did what he always did, which was take care of things for her like he had when she was a child.

They went to the local bank down in the village and offered all the necessary documents.

"You'll have to submit a declaration form with her current address," the bank manager said to Gordon, who put the first deposit in her account. "But once she's approved, you'll be able to start depositing and withdrawing from her account."

She felt like a child sitting there next to her father, letting him do the things a normal adult could do. The bank manager had been treating her like one since he'd heard she was divorced and broke and needed her dad to help her open a bank account.

When they left with an activated debit card, she called her attorney.

"You can let Mr. Moretti's lawyer know my bank account number," she said, beaten down.

"I'll let him know right away," Alicia Sommers said. "Let me know if you need anything else. Anything at all. Call day or night." The best and brightest attorney was making a name for herself by taking Remy on as a client. Her name had already been printed on Page Six about Remy's divorce.

"Thanks." Remy could barely get the word out.

Starting her car, she noticed her gas tank was almost empty.

"Let's go home," she said, disgusted with the state of her life, because where she was going wasn't her home. She had no home. She sat in the parking spot and didn't move. She dropped her head on the steering wheel and said, "What am I doing with my life?"

Gordon turned in his seat to face her. "There's a difference between giving up and knowing when you've had enough."

"I'm a loser," she said, resting her head on the back of the car's leather seat. She held up her bare fingers. "Look at me. I have nothing. No husband. No children. No house. No career. I'm nothing without him. He was right."

All those fights. All those things he said about her. She had no talent. Decorating and drawing were hobbies that children could do. Nothing she did was important. She couldn't even have children without ruining everything. She was too anxious, too nervous, too worrisome, too everything. She couldn't even carry a child to full-term.

"Let's be honest, Remy," Gordon said, in the tone that reminded her even more of being a kid. "Leaving Joe isn't your problem."

"What's my problem, then?" Remy didn't know where her life was going, but leaving Joe had started the downward spiral.

"It's what you think of yourself," Gordon said. "You were an amazing wife and support system for Joe. Yet, you somehow see yourself as inferior to him because you aren't chasing his definition of success."

"I didn't do much of anything." She'd said it so quietly she could barely hear herself. "And look at me now."

Over the past fifteen years, she'd built Joe's life and she hadn't built hers. She had no education besides a twenty-year-old degree in art. What could someone do with an art degree?

"What's that supposed to mean?" Gordon shook his head. "Look at the art auction and what you did for Meredith."

She shrugged. "I had Greg helping me." Her best friend from college had helped her organize the auction, set it up, and had gotten the people to come. "All I did was supply the location and name."

The Moretti name went a long way in Boston. Real estate, construction, and businesses were all part of the Moretti dynasty. Then Joe had started his own financial firm and the name became synonymous with power, wealth, and prestige. Page Six had made it clear that Remy Moretti's decision to leave her husband of fifteen years only meant she'd married him for the status. They had failed to mention how leaving Joe left her with no status.

"You always jumped," Gordon said. "You were always the first one, too."

"What?" Remy asked, not following her father.

"You always jumped in the water, even the coldest Atlantic waters," Gordon said, pointing his finger at her. "Not Meredith. She needed to put a toe in just to make sure, but you'd close your eyes and jump right in."

Remy smiled at her dad. She knew what he was trying to do; find some life metaphor to help her get through this difficult time, but like a belly flop, it fell flat.

Gordon loved her, and that should be enough. She had Meredith to support her. That should be enough. She had a new support group living in Blueberry Bay. That should be enough.

But Remy didn't feel good enough for any of that.

"Thanks, Dad," she said as he patted her arm. She could see the hope in his eyes that he had fixed things. "We should get you home so you can go out for that dinner with Ginny."

"Oh, I don't need to go tonight," he said.

She cocked her head, putting on a big smile. "And what do you plan on eating? The dinner I bought for one?"

"Ah, that's right," Gordon said. "Why don't you come along?"

There was nothing she wanted to do less than go to a spaghetti dinner as a third wheel alongside her father.

"I'm good, thanks. Really," she said when he frowned. "I bought a great dinner, and I just want to watch something mindless."

"Alright, but if you change your mind..." Gordon put on his seat belt. "I'll bring home ice cream."

"I'll let you know," she said, smiling at the sweetness her father still had even after all the trouble she had caused with the divorce. She was sure moving to Maine wasn't his first pick for retirement, but he'd moved to be close to her and Meredith. She knew he missed his friends and the Andover Golf Club. Gordon liked change as much as Meredith did—and she didn't handle change well at all.

"Do you mind stopping at the market?" Gordon asked, completely forgetting her incident earlier, or just not making it a thing.

But it was a thing. She wasn't going back inside that market ever again.

"Sure, Dad, no problem." She pulled out of the parking lot of the bank, following the main road to downtown, where the market was. Right in the heart of Blueberry Bay.

She pulled into a parking space close to the store, just not as close as the always-open spot she used to park in. Now the No Parking sign hung high and clear, like she'd finally found Waldo within the crowd to never unsee him.

"I think I'll stay in the car and try calling Joe again," she said, holding up the phone. She hadn't told Gordon she was blocked yet.

He nodded, unaware of her fib, and took off for the market.

Remy peeked in the rearview at Gordon as he made his way into the store. The red clapboard building sat at the beginning of the opening of the small harbor made by the mouth of the local river coming down from the mountains. She loved the quaintness of the local market, the Maine feeling of its structure—the mighty lobster red symbolized a feeling in her. She loved Maine. It had become her refuge, and she was grateful for its natural beauty, along with the comfortable feeling of being...home.

Maine had become her home, whether these people knew her as the divorcée who lived with her sister and father or some woman who was somehow strangely connected to the crazy artist.

At least she wouldn't be known as Mrs. Joseph Moretti. Now she could be Remy again.

When Joe had shown up at the festival, Remy thought that had meant he wanted to try to make things work. But he hadn't changed his mind about anything. He didn't want to try IVF or even think about adopting or fostering children. He hadn't changed his mind about her working or getting a job outside of the family business when the opportunity had arisen to teach with Greg at the local adult education program through a small museum. He wanted her to be available for him and only him.

Remy could no longer give up her own life when he offered nothing to her but things.

And she didn't want any of it. Not the fancy cars or the houses or the expensive lifestyle. She didn't need name brand clothes or designer handbags. She didn't want jewelry or the vacations. All of that was just stuff. She wanted a husband and a family.

And she wouldn't waste any more time being with someone who didn't want that, too.

She wanted more in life, and for that, she wouldn't apologize. Joe could make her suffer for wanting what he'd promised when he proposed. That's why she didn't have a problem giving back the ring. She wanted nothing to do with his empty promises.

When the car door opened, she sat up, ready to start the car, when Gordon leaned into the car. "Guess who's looking for some help during the spring and summer seasons!"

He stepped away from the car to let a man lean down, and that's when she saw Emil's son. His eyes widened when he recognized her sitting in the driver's seat.

"She's your daughter?" he said, not hiding his surprise.

She couldn't believe this. "Dad? What are you doing?"

"You love the market, and they're looking for someone who can help." Gordon opened the door wider as if that would change Colby's hesitation to look inside at his daughter.

"We're looking for counter help," Colby said. A half grin, half scowl grew on his lips as though he knew what she knew. She wasn't taking the job.

"I'm good, thanks," she said, looking away from them.

But Gordon wasn't having it. "This would be perfect for you!" he said. Then he turned back to Colby. "She just needs something for the time being. Until she finds what she's looking for."

"And what's that?" Colby asked.

Remy looked at Gordon, hoping he had the answer.

Gordon smiled at her. "She just needs a new adventure."

"Adventure?" Colby said with a chuckle. "Well, I can promise some adventure."

Remy shook her head. "No, no, no. I'm sorry, but my father misspoke when he said I wanted a job. I'm looking for something more than a counter helper."

This made Colby's lips fall into a flat line. He let out a single condescending laugh, which made Gordon give her a look as though she were the one being rude. "Right, well, you do like expensive wine."

Her mouth dropped at the comment. How dare he judge her? Who was this man? And why did he have to look so hot while being a jerk?

Remy was done with arrogant men. "Have a nice day, Mr. St. Germain."

She wouldn't be rude, but she wasn't sticking around to be insulted again.

"Oh, I will now," he said, turning on his heels with that smirk that made him look like a soap opera bad guy—completely irritating and intriguing at the same time.

Gordon got into the car and didn't say anything for a while as they drove to the house.

"I'm sorry," she said. "I just don't like that guy for some reason."

Gordon shook his head. "I know this is hard."

"What?" She squeezed the wheel. "I'm not being picky. I just need something that will pay more than minimum wage."

"I know that you lived a very lavish lifestyle, and it must be scary to have that ripped out from underneath you."

"You have no idea." She'd said it too quickly. No way to take it back.

"I do, actually," Gordon said. "I know what it's like to be broke, and I also know what it's like to have too much. Neither is easy."

"Dad, I'm not a snob. It's just not the kind of work I'm looking for," she said.

"Sometimes it's about being busy, not the work," Gordon said. "I meant it when I said you needed an adventure. You need to get out, meet people. What better place than the market in town? You're great with people."

"Well, some people," Remy said, thinking about lumberjack man.

"You'd be great there, helping people choose their wine with their fish."

She was good at pairing wine with fish and other types of flavors. She had a real talent for throwing an exquisite dinner party. She wasn't a snob. It was just what she knew. She knew expensive tastes.

But wasn't that the definition of a snob?

"I understand you don't want to work there, but there is something out there for you. You just have to get out there to find it," Gordon said. He acted like finding a job at forty-five after not working for fifteen years would be like choosing fish at the market, or maybe he knew this was the best she could get.

The truth hit her. She needed to take whatever she could.

"Maybe I should apply," she said. "Get something on my resume."

"Just get your own money," Gordon said. "Something that man can't get his hands on."

When she pulled up to the house, she couldn't believe she was about to do what she was about to do. "Do you think you'll be okay if I just drop you off?"

Gordon smiled. "Sure."

"I'm going to head back to the market and ask if they'd like my help," she said.

Gordon nodded. "Sounds great."

CHAPTER 4

*N*ever in a million years would Colby believe that high-society Ms. Boston would actually take the job at a fish market, but there she was standing with his sister up front at the counter.

"Have you used one of these before?" Bridgette said to Remy as she pointed to the card machine they had just recently purchased. It was a polite question, since clearly Remy didn't know what she was doing.

Remy shook her head. "I'm afraid I haven't worked a cash register in years."

He groaned. His father's "favorite" customer was now their newest charity case.

Apparently, Ms. Boston had no prior work experience except for being a housewife. His father hadn't even asked for references. Not that working a register or helping customers around the small market would be difficult work, but it was more about work ethic really. Did she show up on time? Was she polite to customers? Was she a team player?

He didn't want to train a spoiled woman from the city.

If it were up to him, he'd deal without having someone at the counter and figure things out. He could take a break from fishing, he supposed. Let his sternman, Kevin, run the traps for a couple of months. The market was dead slow at that point in the spring season anyway, and they wouldn't need any help.

If only his sister's baby was coming a few weeks earlier.

He sighed thinking of his baby sister, Bridgette.

"Do you need anything?" he asked his sister, who at eight months pregnant looked like she was about to pop.

She shook her head. "I'm good."

He didn't even make eye contact with the newest employee. Maybe fishing for lobsters all year wasn't such a bad idea.

Groaning to himself at the thought of another summer not being out on the water, he walked out back to where his father cut and sliced up fish for local vendors.

"Can I help before I head out?" he asked Emil.

"No, I'm good here." His father rested from cutting for a second and looked out at the floor of the market. "She's going to be great, that one."

"Ms. Riesling is going to be great?" Colby said with an eye roll.

Emil smiled. "Your mother thinks very highly of her and her sister."

Colby didn't understand the fanfare for the newcomers. What they had done for the little village of Blueberry Bay, allowing the Queen Bees to continue working in the fields after their father died, had been kind. He didn't deny that. But he just thought that Remy in particular was a snob. And that's all there was to it.

He had waited on enough out-of-towners to know this woman was only in Blueberry Bay because of circumstance, but she would hightail it as soon as her situation turned around. High-society people who came to seaside towns like Blueberry Bay came for its quaintness and seaside charm, not the locals. They kept up formalities, and summer people tended to keep to themselves and not help the locals with their troubles.

And quaint seaside villages had plenty of troubles.

"Have you talked to Sadie this morning?" Emil asked.

Colby shut his eyes, dreading the next part of this conversation. "No, why?"

"She said Brynn was calling her last night," Emil said.

Speaking of troubles.

Colby's head dropped, automatically spiraling at all the things his sister would say to her daughter. "What did she say?"

Emil shook his head. "She didn't talk to her."

"That's a relief," Colby said, praying it would stay that way. "No good will come from them communicating until she gets the help she needs."

Until Sadie's mother followed through on her end, Colby wasn't budging, no matter how much she promised to stay clean.

His sister always broke her promises.

Colby left after that and parked his truck down at the harbor. He'd unload some of the traps he needed to repair. Maybe Sadie would like to help him and make some extra money. Didn't she want to go to that basketball game with him in Portland?

He wondered how Sadie felt about Brynn calling. It had been hard enough losing her father like she had, but now her mother coming back into her life after all the times she'd left for nothing more than to get high?

He'd never let Sadie go through that again, no matter what.

He pulled out his phone and dialed the one guy he knew who could help him.

"I know, I know," Quinn said, answering the phone. "I totally bailed on poker, but next week I promise I'll be there."

"I'm not calling about poker." Colby hated the fact that he used his friend for this kind of stuff. "Brynn's calling Sadie again."

"When did she call?" Quinn said, getting professional right away.

"I'm not sure," he said. "I haven't talked to Sadie about it. She's in school."

"Do you want me to call the police?" Quinn, the attorney, said. "She's breaking her restraining order."

"Yeah, I think we need to give them a call." Colby hated the idea of having the police in their family affairs. Fishermen didn't like to involve anyone other than their own. But what else could he do? Sadie needed protection from her mom right now. He didn't know what Brynn was up to.

"I'll do that right away," Quinn said. "But could you do one thing for me?"

"Name it." Colby didn't need to hear what Quinn had to say. He'd do anything for his friend.

"Be good to Remy," Quinn said. "She's going through a lot right now and I'd hate for my good friend to be a thorn in my girlfriend's sister's side."

"She said I was a thorn?" Colby was already annoyed. "What did she say?"

"She told her sister how embarrassed she was when she found out her ex-husband had cut off her credit card and you made a comment about her expensive wine," Quinn said.

Colby hadn't realized her situation. "She thought she was too good to work in the market, and I just pointed out that she could afford expensive wine and probably needed a higher paying job."

"She's going through a really hard time right now," Quinn said, now his friend.

"But she can read though, right?" Colby almost started to tell Quinn the story of her parking in the loading parking spot but changed his mind when he heard Quinn moan after Colby's rhetorical question.

"Come on, man. Be nice, at least," Quinn said.

"Fine, I'll play nice." Colby climbed out of his truck, grumbling quietly to himself about being nice. He decided to change the subject. "Do you think Kyle would want to fix up some of my traps?"

"Sure," Quinn said. "He's just about finished with baseball. Drop them off at the house anytime."

"Great, I'll do that," Colby said. "By the way, Tony called you a chicken last night."

"Whatever, he doesn't even know how to play poker," Quinn said.

"He did pretty well," Colby egged on his friend, who was as competitive as him. "You better show up next time."

"I will," Quinn said. "I promise."

But Colby didn't hold his breath. His friend was iffy at best on good days. As a single parent, Quinn had to put his son first, Colby knew. He understood how hard it was to raise a child alone, just by helping like he did with Sadie. His parents couldn't do it all. Nor should they have to continue raising their child's child after raising their own. This was the time they should be enjoying life, not running around trying to raise a teenage girl.

A call beeped through. "Quinn, I got to take this call. It's the school."

"Sure thing," Quinn said. "I'll head down to the station right now."

"Great, thanks, man," Colby said, then he switched lines. "Hello, Colby St. Germain."

"Mr. St. Germain?" the voice said on the other line. "This is Nancy McCarthy, the nurse over at Blueberry Bay Middle School."

Colby's stomach dropped, and he stopped in his tracks on the dock. "Yes?"

"I'm calling to let you know that Miss Sadie needs a change of clothing and she would like it to be handled discreetly."

"Excuse me?" he asked. "Is everything okay?"

"Yes, everything's just fine. It's just that Sadie . . .became a woman today," the older woman said. "And you need to bring in some clothing for her."

Colby stared at his boat. "Right. I'll be there as soon as I can."

"Oh, and Mr. St. Germain, the school can provide her with some feminine products," the nurse said. "But you may want to stop at a store to pick up some more comfortable products."

Colby just stared ahead, praying he wouldn't have to ask his mother, who had just turned seventy, if she still had feminine products lying around.

"Thank you, Mrs. McCarthy," he said, to the same nurse he had while in middle school. "I'll be there as soon as I can."

He didn't bother grabbing any of the traps from the boat. He'd have to come back later. Sadie needed him way more than the traps did.

But he stopped the truck before he left downtown. He needed to go back to the market and pick up some supplies for her first. Or maybe he should bring her?

He'd get his sister. Bridgette would know what to do.

Colby ran inside the market to find Emil behind the counter with Remy.

"Where's Bridgette?" he asked, looking around the store.

"She's gone," Emil said.

"She was here just a few minutes ago," Colby said.

"Well, we've got things under control here. Remy is a natural." Emil turned to Remy and gave her a wink. "Bridgette was tired, so I sent her home."

"We just opened the store. How is she tired?" he asked.

"I'm guessing you've never been eight months pregnant," Remy said from behind the counter.

He pursed his lips closed so he wouldn't say something rude.

"I need her," he said. "It's about Sadie."

"Sadie?" Emil said, worry now flashing across his face. "What's going on with Sadie?"

Colby dropped his head, wishing he wouldn't have to tell his father about his niece's first day of becoming a woman.

"Let's just say I need Bridgette." He hoped his father would take the hint. "You can't help with this kind of thing."

But Emil didn't.

"I bet if you just tell me what it is, I can help." Emil looked at Remy.

"I need to buy her feminine products." There, Colby said it.

Emil's face dropped. "Oh."

Colby gave his father a nod in agreement about how uncomfortable they both felt, then began walking toward the aisle where they carried very few products. His dad came with him.

"She's at school?" Remy said from behind, following the two.

Colby ignored her as Emil answered her. "Yes."

Both men stopped in front of the small spot where they carried feminine products and froze.

"Is this all you carry?" Remy's nose wrinkled like she smelled something rotten.

"Not too many people come into the market to buy feminine products," Colby said.

"Probably because you don't carry anything." She picked up a small blue box of tampons.

Colby looked at his father, who looked back at him. He wished she'd just butt out of their private family conversation.

"I'm going to run to the store," Colby said, but his feet didn't move toward the door.

"Maybe you should check Bridgette's desk," Emil said. "She'll have some things."

"She's eight months pregnant," Remy said, as though that idea was the stupidest idea she had ever heard of. "She's not going to have those kinds of supplies for a young girl. I mean, I'm guessing she's young?"

Colby stared at her, not answering because he wasn't sure how to answer. This was the woman who had once complained they didn't have the right type of wine to go with the fish they sold. This was the woman who always enjoyed pointing out things around the market they could improve on with sentences like, "It's a shame you don't have doors with windows so the customers can see from outside," or "It's too bad the market doesn't carry fresher produce."

"Yes, just turned thirteen," Emil said.

Remy plucked the blue box from Colby's hand and put it back onto the shelf. "Let me go to the store."

Colby turned to Remy, realizing he had two choices. He could let go of his annoyance and let this woman help, or he could bother his eight-month pregnant sister and ask her to help.

"That would be wonderful!" Emil answered.

"What pant size is your daughter?" Remy asked Colby.

Colby shook his head. "She's not my daughter. She's my niece."

"Oh," she said, with the same face she had made upon finding out they didn't carry French cheese. "So do you know how tall she is?"

"She's almost five feet. She's probably a small?" he answered, not really sure. He had never picked the clothes. He just paid for them.

"Like a small?" Remy's eyebrows lifted high on her forehead. Then she clapped her hands together and said, "Okay, well, then I'll be right back."

He quickly pulled out his wallet from his back pocket. "Wait, here's some cash." He pulled out a couple of twenties.

She stared at it at first, then plucked it from his hands. "Right."

He hated that when she walked away, he couldn't help but take a glance at her. There was no denying Remy's beauty. He still remembered the first time she had walked into the market this past summer. He'd thought she was one of the most beautiful women he had ever laid eyes on. But then she had opened her mouth. The first thing she'd said when she had inspected his family's store was that they needed better lighting.

But as he and his father watched her walk down the road and get into her car, he had to admit that what she was doing was kinder than her usual self.

"How lucky that she started when she did," Emil said.

Colby wouldn't go that far. "Of all the people to hire, I don't know why you picked her."

"What people?" Emil said. "We had no other applicants."

This surprised Colby. "Really?"

"The college kids haven't come home yet and the summer workers haven't come up from the south, and most people around Blueberry Bay don't want to work in a market. I'm surprised she does."

That he would agree on.

In less than ten minutes, Remy came back with two bags in her hands. She handed him the first bag. "Here you are."

He opened it up and saw pink boxes labeled as maxi pads, flushable wipes, and a perfumed body spray.

From the other bag, she pulled out a pair of black pants. She folded the black pants up and put them into a small beach bag with draw straps. Then she opened the pink box and pulled out four maxi pads and put them inside, along with the wipes and spray. The last item she took out was a big chocolate bar and she put it inside, tightening the draw straps and handed it over.

"Here." She stepped back.

"Thank you," Colby said, his eyes meeting hers. For a split second, the cornelian eyes warmed, and he could see what his father always said when she left the market—she was beautiful. A classical kind of beauty one didn't see too often nowadays. The kind of beauty that didn't use make-up or fillers or filters, just her smile. And as posh and fancy as she had entered Blueberry Bay, he could see a very slight change in the stranger since arriving.

"Is she at school with the nurse?" Remy asked.

He nodded. "Yeah, I think so."

"The nurse will help her," Remy said. "Then Sadie's mom can take it from there."

Colby shot a look at Emil, praying he would stay quiet. But Emil couldn't help himself. His father liked this woman.

"Unfortunately, Sadie's mom is unable to care for her," he chimed in.

Remy's mouth opened in silent shock.

"I should go," Colby said.

"It's none of my business, but…" Remy began to say to him as he walked away.

Colby shut his eyes, silently sighing to himself as he waited for the criticism she was about to divulge to him.

"When I became a woman," she continued, "my mom took me out of school for the day. She made it a big deal like it was something really special—like becoming part of a club. She took me out to a fancy lunch and bought me a gift—a little charm bracelet that I still have."

He waited at the door and turned around, mostly to be polite but also curious about what she had to say.

"It's scary and gross, so taking her home just to clean up and stuff is also nice," she said. She gave him a smile as she walked back to the counter.

He almost couldn't believe it, but that was really good advice. "Thanks for your help. We're completely clueless, obviously."

He held up the bag for Sadie, and just as he was about to ask what charms her mother had gotten her, a customer walked in and grabbed Remy's attention, who greeted her right away.

"Good morning, welcome to Harbor Market," Remy said.

As Remy helped the customer, Colby suddenly noticed he was staring at her, and a sensation rippled throughout his body as he turned away, flushed.

Whatever that was, he didn't like it. He didn't like it at all.

CHAPTER 5

*T*he sounds of the waves woke Remy from her sleep. The pounding against the granite shoreline below was much stronger than usual, especially when compared to the gentle noise she'd fallen asleep to the night before. She sat up in bed, the sun just poking up from the dark horizon. The sky was tinged with deep pinks and lavender against the flat-lined clouds.

Pink skies in the morning, sailor's warning, she thought of the old saying about the seas.

Spending a whole winter in Blueberry Bay had taught Remy three things—

The sound of the waves forecasted weather changes before you saw the changes.

Flat-lined clouds predicted really bad weather.

And no matter how clear blue the sky and how bright the sun, it could change within a heartbeat.

Before she went downstairs, she dug through her box of jewelry, looking for her charm bracelet from when she was a girl. When she found it, she held each tiny charm in her fingers, thinking back to each one and when she'd gotten them. Some for her birthdays, others for big moments like her sweet sixteen, her confirmation, and graduation. She had stopped wearing it once she'd gone away to college, replacing it with fancier, more expensive jewelry. She slipped it onto her wrist, still fitting perfectly.

She decided to take her coffee to the beach and write in her journal. Her daily routine since she was ten, she took her tiny notebooks everywhere and wrote down everything. Not that she thought any of her words were important, but it had been her way of communicating all her big emotions as a little girl. On her tenth birthday, her mother had given her the first diary. At first, it was just a place to write about boyfriends and fights with her friends at school, but as middle school problems became bigger high school problems, she continued to write on a regular basis.

Now, she needed her writing more than ever.

She had thought about burning them, especially the years she'd wasted with Joe. Throwing them all into a fire along the beach or maybe making some raft to burn in the sea like the Vikings did for ceremonial funerals.

Because leaving Joe felt like a death.

Leaving her life behind, all the people and friends, the time and work she had given to their life, all to be taken away.

She hadn't missed the irony that she'd left Joe because he wouldn't have children with her, and now she wouldn't be able to afford children without him. Not on the pathetic wage she earned at the market. How is anyone able to live on minimum wage?

Maybe she deserved it. Maybe she didn't need to be a mother.

But she knew deep in her soul that was all she'd ever wanted to be—a mother. Anyone's mother.

She wanted to settle down. She wanted to live down the street from her parents and sister and raise her children together as a big cohesive family. She wanted to have the pounding of little feet inside her house. She wanted to watch her child grow and help guide them. She wanted to pick them up at school and ask who they sat with at lunch. She wanted to tuck someone in at night and read them a story. She wanted to love someone more than herself.

She didn't want to bounce from one house to the other for just long enough to unpack anymore. She wanted roots, stability, family around her, and a family of her own.

When she'd first met Joe, he had wanted that too. But when things had gotten harder and she wasn't getting pregnant, his interest faded. When she'd miscarried, Joe had been supportive, but after the second, he'd told her he was done.

"What about adopting?" she'd said. "We have so much."

"To give all I've earned to someone that's not mine?" he had said, shaking his head. "No, I'd rather give it to my brother's son."

She had stared at him. "Your brother's son? What about your nieces and other nephew?"

He'd scrunched his brows together as though she were being ludicrous to think her sister's children, who had known Joe their whole lives as their uncle and was even her nephew's godfather, would inherit some of Joe's fortune. Did he ever consider them family?

"Or your wife?" she'd asked, wondering what his will looked like. Joe was fifteen years her senior. It was a possibility he might die before her. Would she inherit his wealth, or was she out of the will, like her sister's kids?

"Don't be ridiculous, Remy," he'd said, not answering.

That was the fight that had started it. The beginning of the end.

And like a curtain being pulled back, the shiny, clean, pressed exterior of Joe could no longer cover up the things she had ignored before. Joe's lifestyle had no longer been enough for Remy. She wanted more. Lonely dinners, empty beds, house parties full of people she didn't know—she no longer wanted that.

Remy had planned on leaving Joe before her sister had inherited the cottage—it had only been a matter of days.

She had really thought he understood where she stood when he'd arrived at the festival.

How had she been so wrong?

She pushed away the words he'd said to her when he'd left the cottage. She needed them out of her head. She didn't want to start her day like that.

She grabbed her small notebook and special pen and stuffed them into her fanny pack, then poured her coffee into a traveler's mug and headed out toward the small footpath that hugged the edge of the Atlantic Ocean.

Her hair flew across her face as she stepped out onto the porch, whipping around.

There's most definitely going to be a storm, she thought to herself, not even having to hear the weather report.

The waves crashed against the hard rocks lining the sugar-sand beach. With the tide all the way in, Remy had to sit on her favorite rock, perched over what her sister named Queens' Beach.

Thinking of the Queens, Remy remembered that their monthly meeting would be tomorrow evening. She hadn't seen many of the Queen Bees over the winter, since many of them traveled to Florida or somewhere warmer than Maine's blue-berry coast.

Even Ginny had gone for a few weeks while Gordon went golfing in the Outer Banks.

Remy had stayed all winter. The days had blurred together from one day to the next, and here she was, literally stuck between a rock and a cottage. Should she go back? Joe would forget everything he had texted. She could just go back, and everything would be just the way it was.

She wrote in her journal on the next clean page, listing all the things that would happen if she went back.

No children.

No family.

No suburb community.

No pets.

Remy tapped her pen against the paper and watched the waves slap the rock's surface. Leaping into the air, droplets of water danced through the air. Like a star or a fingerprint or a seashell, each droplet and each spray of water was unique. She was surprised she loved the water so much. The softest, smoothest element on earth, yet it could be the most dangerous and destructive.

She thought of the storm that had killed eight men at sea years ago. The Storm of the Century they had called it, but Remy thought of it as the storm of death. Eight families never able to recover their loved ones' bodies. Only one survivor—her sister's father, Jacob O'Neill.

Jacob had never recovered after that. Her mother had said he couldn't sleep without waking up in night terrors, screaming for air, crying for his life. He'd recovered using medication, and when that had worn out, he'd used alcohol, or worse. Her mother had left Jacob when Meredith was four, when things got really bad. Gordon helped them when they came to the city and soon her parents fell in love.

She started tracing out the silhouette of the bare tree line along the bay with a piece of charcoal from the last campfire they had this winter. Remy smiled at the memory. Meredith had forced everyone out in the snow to watch a snowstorm roll out to sea. Everyone grumbled about having to go out in the cold, but no one really complained, because they all loved Meredith. They all loved what she did for them. And it turned out to be one of the best nights Remy had in a long time.

Meredith saved Remy that winter. If she hadn't had her sister, she wasn't sure if she'd be lost in that ocean right now. She had been so low after the festival, so broken about the divorce, it was as if her heart was being dragged under the water, along the ocean floor, and crashing into the rocks over and over again.

She never wanted to leave Joe, but he didn't want to change.

Maybe she was to blame for everything falling apart. Joe certainly blamed her. He didn't understand her need to have a child.

What if he has a child with another woman like Phillip had done to Meredith?

She stopped sketching as a colder wind swooped through, lifting up the pages of the notebook as she held them down. She needed to come up with a plan. Something to clear her mind. No more moping around.

She had the meeting for the Queen Bees. She looked forward to seeing all the women again. She saw the usuals, like Ginny, Hazel, and Carolyn on a regular basis. They'd formed a little coffee klatch with Meredith and her. Each afternoon, after a stroll through the fields and then a three-mile power walk, the ladies met for coffee and blueberry cake. She missed the snow-birds and couldn't wait to hear all their stories, but deep down, she knew Blueberry Bay wasn't her community. It was Meredith's.

The cottage was hers. The beach Remy sat at was hers. Remy was a guest and a guest of the community. Until she bought something or found a rental she could afford, she was considered homeless.

Homeless.

She needed to make a list.

Find a home.

Find a better job.

Start something to refocus her thoughts.

She inhaled the dampness in the air that hinted at spring's arrival. Looking back out at the water, she noticed the waves had picked up, even since she had first arrived at the beach.

She stood up, grabbing her coffee and notebook. As the wind blew around her, the waves crashing against the cliffs drowned out her thoughts. She looked out and noticed a piece of drift-wood tumbling in and out of a small cove, unable to get stuck or get out of the treacherous waves pounding against the granite. She felt like that log. Unable to anchor down but also unable to free herself.

"Remy!" called out a voice from afar.

Remy turned to see a figure coming from the other end of the beach. "Ginny? Dad?"

"What are you doing all the way out on those rocks?" Ginny yelled from the path, not getting closer.

Gordon waved her up. "Come on this side of the path."

Suddenly, a wave slammed up the rocks and doused her with water. Remy noticed the sandy path she had used to get to the rock she sat on was no longer there but covered by the ocean. Then another wave came pounding in after that, spraying her face, startling her.

She immediately backed off the ledge and began to climb back up the hill.

"You have to be careful when weather comes in fast like this," Ginny said, looking at her watch. "I bet there will be snow by noon."

"But the snow just melted," Remy complained. It had already been a long winter.

"Looks like a doozy too," Ginny said. "You should probably hit the grocery store."

That must be a New England thing.

"I used to work at a market when I was a kid," Remy said, suddenly remembering her first job in her hometown. A big-chain superstore unlike the quaint Harbor Market. It had everything one could imagine in the way of food, supplies and other random items. "Storms always brought in panicked customers."

"Better to be safe and have cookie supplies than sorry," Ginny said, giving Remy a wink. "But I do love a snow day."

Remy smiled, wishing she could afford to buy all the snow-storm supplies she used to with her nieces and nephew. When a big storm would come through, she'd drive up to her parents' and bake all day with her mom. Meredith would walk over with her kids, and they'd all hang out in the kitchen, gossiping and watching daytime soap operas. She'd loved that time more than ever.

Now she had an old piece of fish and a very expensive bottle of wine.

A pretty pathetic snow day.

"I better hurry ahead," Remy said to Gordon and Ginny. "I have to get to work."

"Tell Emil and everyone I said hello," Ginny said happily.

Remy nodded and kissed her dad on the cheek. "I'll see you later."

"Sure thing," Gordon said back.

Remy hurried ahead, not really in a rush to get to work, since she didn't start until the afternoon. She just needed to clear her head. As she reached the cottage, she looked through the window and saw Meredith sitting at the piano with Quinn next to her on the bench. She couldn't hear the music, but she didn't need to; she knew it was something beautiful. Something that captivated Quinn. The look of pure amazement on his face said it all.

Remy unlocked her car with her phone and got inside. Her keys already in the cup holder ready for her to escape. She drove a lot these days. Anywhere that didn't have happy couples.

Before she knew it, she was parked in front of the market as the snow started to fall. Her silly luxury car could hardly handle the main roads when it started to snow, and storms coming off the ocean was a whole other story. She would have to walk home after work.

"What are you doing here so early?" Emil said as she walked in, shaking off the fat flakes that had clung to her on the short walk from her car.

"I thought I'd get here before it got worse," she lied, but Emil seemed pleased by her answer.

"Now that's a dedicated employee," he said.

She smiled, walking to the back to put her coat and purse away. She grabbed the apron—the only uniform requirement—and walked to the counter, noticing Emil was all alone.

"Is Bridgette still not feeling well?" she asked.

"She's in labor!" Emil said with gusto.

Remy worried for a second that this might not be good and frowned. "Isn't she only eight months?"

Emil smiled, clasping his hands together. "The doctors think she and the baby are going to be just fine, and I'm going to be a granddad for a second time!"

But Remy didn't share his excitement. She wouldn't get excited until the baby was born alive and healthy. That's when she would celebrate. "Good thing I came in," she said. "I wish you had called me. I would've come earlier."

Emil shook his head. "She's with her mother. Besides, I'm in good hands with Colby here today."

Remy didn't want to ask, but she had noticed he didn't say anything about the baby's father.

As if he could read her mind, Emil said, "Her husband's out at sea, in the Navy. Isn't able to come home for the birth now that the baby's early. He planned to take time off in a month."

Suddenly, Colby appeared out of nowhere.

"I meant to call you. But you don't have to work today," Colby said. "We'll probably close due to the storm."

Remy's stomach twisted at the thought of losing a whole day's pay. "Really?"

"Not too many customers are going to trek outside this afternoon," Colby said, gesturing his hand toward the front doors. Snow already fell at a fast pace, covering the sidewalks but still melting on the street. "It's going to be ugly out there."

She pursed her lips into a thin line, unable to say the real reason why she was upset they were closing. She needed those hours. "Well, it's just that you're one of the only markets for a few miles. People may need items."

"Doesn't look like they're banging down the doors," Colby said condescendingly, gesturing his hands to the empty market.

"Maybe they don't come because you don't carry much," Remy said, looking around at the sparse, mismatched store items. "You have all this space. You really should start thinking about offering what the town needs."

Colby shot his father a look.

Emil spoke before Colby did. "This used to be just a lobster market up until a few years ago."

Remy could see the customers' confusion. The fish counter carried some of the area's most expensive fish, dropped inside what felt like a gas station market. None of the other items were appealing to people of Blueberry Bay or the tourists that visited. They carried lots of random items and brands.

Remy slowly made her way back behind the counter, hoping her argument might get them to stay open until at least half of her shift was over. "I totally don't mind just staying open by myself if you're worried about the weather."

"We're not worried about the weather. There's just no one who's going to come—"

The bell to the front door rang out and two customers walked in, one right after another.

"You guys still open, Emil?" an older gentleman asked.

"For now," Emil said, nodding at Remy.

"What can I help you with?" she asked.

"We're trying to stock up before the storm hits," one of the men said. "Jane closed up her store early to get home."

"Clam chowder is perfect for this kind of day," she said, wishing they carried fresh supplies other than a lot of fish.

She looked around the market. The whole thing could be so touristy Maine that they'd make a killing. If they just beefed up their product selection and carried great fresh produce, posh products that people wanted but didn't purchase unless on vacation, and a really good selection of alcohol. Who wanted to drink cheap beer on the beach or in their rented cottage? Or while stuck inside during a snowstorm?

"Goes great with a chilled white wine." Remy couldn't bring herself to say the brand name. They really carried terrible names.

"Too bad there isn't good bread," the other guy said.

"I know," she agreed. "Or local potatoes."

Remy noticed Colby scowl at that one. But if he didn't know

what his business was missing, maybe she should point that out. She was their clientele, after all, not the locals that could catch their own fish.

The market needed a new identity, not to be stuck in the past.

The first thing she'd do is bring in local suppliers. Like blueberries for instance. The Queen Bees could sell their honey and a ton of other local products that tourists loved. Baked goods sold at the counter, artisan goods sold as tourist gifts, items one would need for the beach or a stay in a hotel or cottage for vacation. Local craft beers and wine. Churned cheeses made from neighboring farms. A small but smart offering of outfitters' clothing for their stay. All things people from the suburbs and city imagined Maine to sell. Like fresh baked breads and potatoes with their lobster.

And maybe get rid of the feminine supplies.

A few more customers came in, local business owners talking to Emil. Some reopening from the winter.

"I would've stayed in Florida had I known it wasn't done snowing," one of the women said to Colby, who had brooded all day about this or that.

First, Colby complained about the lack of organization the store had. Colby wasn't wrong, the place did have a very strange way of using its space. Shelving units were pushed up against the walls, which made the space big and open, but the few items they did carry got crowded when more than one customer stood in front of them. But whether the shelves were organized well or not, the whole place needed a makeover. Its organization was the least of their problems.

Then, Colby shoveled. He shoveled the front sidewalk, then the back, then around the market. He'd come in, complain about the cold, the amount falling, and shoveling. Then he'd go right back outside.

"What do you like to listen to?" she asked Emil, finding a radio in the back.

"Something soft and quiet," he said.

She picked classical.

"Ah, Chopin," Emil said, recognizing the composer.

She smiled back at him as he turned the volume up a bit more. She grabbed the mop, then all the cleaning supplies she could and headed out front. As customers came and went, she cleaned, finding herself happy to do mindless tasks. She pulled all the items off the shelves and wiped them down and placed them back how she thought things could go. She didn't think Emil would mind, and she doubted Colby would notice the different placements.

She washed the windows, wishing it wasn't snowing so she could clean the outside as well.

"Mind if I pull the shelves from the windows to finish cleaning them?" she asked, wondering why Emil would even think of putting shelves against the windows. "It's such a shame to cover up the view."

"I used to have more refrigerators," Emil said. "Here in the center."

Emil pointed to the center of the room that sat empty and bare.

"What were they for?" she asked.

"People used to travel all the way up here to buy fish, but now with the way shipping goes, I don't need the in-house stock," Emil said.

"You should pull theses shelves out," she said, wanting to do it right then. It made sense. Less people crowding on space.

"Where would you put them?" he asked her.

"In the middle, so people can walk around both sides," she said.

"Wouldn't that make it more crowded?" He shook his head at the thought.

But the more she cleaned and rearranged, the more she just didn't understand the local market at all. Sure, it had a little bit of everything, but even when she'd been a good paying customer who had frequented the establishment, she never left with much of anything.

"Do you still have those refrigerators?"

"We do somewhere in storage," Emil answered.

If Remy owned the place, she'd keep the back as a fish market but the rest as a high-end tourist market. Like you'd see in the city, but with a coastal Maine vibe. She'd open a prepared-foods area to make the chowders and the clam bakes, along with charcuterie boards on beautiful pottery and ingredients from local farms.

She'd take the shelves from the walls and let the room speak for itself—the market's heritage in its hand-painted signs for lobster, haddock, and cod on the walls.

"How long have you owned this place?" she asked, removing the last of the stuff from a shelf against the far wall.

"Forever," Emil said, now helping her remove the items. It had been at least a half hour since a customer had come in. Snow continued to fall outside. "Shouldn't you head home?"

She waved Emil off. "I'm fine."

"Dad," Colby said, coming in from outside. "Bridgette had the baby."

"Oh, that's great news!" Emil stopped what he was doing and headed toward the back. "I'm headed to the hospital right now."

"What is it?" she asked Colby, hoping this would change his sour attitude. "A boy or a girl?"

"A girl," he said. "Camden."

"Oh, I love that name!" she exclaimed, maybe a bit overboard, but it was better than how she really felt, which was sad for some reason. "And healthy?"

He nodded. "Everything looks good."

She smiled at that and then noticed Colby staring at her. She looked away, worried she had given away her real feelings, which was more than just a little sad but also a bit jealous and ashamed for being jealous.

She should just go.

"I can close up," she said. "You two should head to the hospital before it gets too dangerous to drive."

"That's really kind of you. Are you sure?" Emil asked.

"Yes, of course. Not much to it," she said, shrugging. This only made Colby grimace.

"I'll have to wait until Sadie's dismissed from school," Colby said.

Remy was surprised they still had school. Where she grew up, they'd cancel the night before if there were any snow predictions in the forecast.

"They haven't closed school yet?" She looked out the windows. Snow fell in a steady rhythm.

"They usually try to get through lunch before any early release," Colby said, looking at his phone. "Speak of the devil. I better head over there."

"I'm good," she said to both men. "If you leave the keys, I can lock up the place and put them somewhere you'd like."

"Ah, I don't know," Colby said, clearly not trusting her.

She wasn't completely offended…but offended nonetheless. What would she steal from this market?

"I'll be fine," she said, taking the keys from Emil's hand. "What could happen?"

CHAPTER 6

*A*fter the hospital, Colby brought Sadie home and headed back to the store. The snow still fell at a steady speed, and if he didn't keep up with the parking lot, it would take forever to clean up when this mess was over.

When he pulled onto Main Street, sitting in the loading parking space was Remy's car...again. Why did she move her car from the correct parking space to the loading space? And why wasn't she home? It had been hours since they'd left for the hospital, and she was supposed to close up. The snow now fell at a speed that no one should be driving in without a plow attached to their truck like his. She'd be a fool if she drove her sedan home.

He parked right in front and saw that all the lights were on in the store. Through the windows, he could see her on her hands and knees. Was there a bottle of wine next to her?

He moaned to himself, hoping this wasn't going to end up in a messier situation than there was outside. He jumped out of his truck and opened the front door to the store, stomping to get the snow off his boots, while also letting her know he was there.

She popped her head up and he noticed a bucket behind her.

"Did you know these shelves could be so clean?" she said,

rubbing a cloth against the shelving's leg. The commercial shelving may have been on wheels, but that didn't mean they wanted them moved.

"What are you doing?" he asked.

She put the cloth down and stood up, leaving the glass of wine on the floor. "Well, I had nothing to do tonight, so I thought I'd finish cleaning the shelves."

He looked at the floor, which was filled with all the items. It would take forever to put everything back.

"Did my dad ask you to do all this?" He was completely baffled by this woman. Did she expect him to pay her for doing something no one told her to do?

"No, but you complained about how everything was disorganized, so I created a design of how grocery stores and other markets carry their items with your own items and...here."

She picked up a notebook from the floor and showed it to him. Before he looked at the page, he noticed the whole wall of shelves had been moved from one side of the store to the opposite one.

"Did you move all the shelves?" he asked, absolutely mystified by the audacity of this woman. "Are you kidding me right now?"

"Are you kidding me?" she asked him. She pointed to the wall. "You have an original mural by Jacob O'Neill, and you have shelving in front of it?"

He looked at the wall. He had forgotten about the mural that had been painted years ago.

"That's Jacob O'Neill's?" he asked. He had recently heard about the crazy old man that lived on the cliffs had been some famous painter.

She marched over to the bottom corner of the painting and pointed to a mermaid. "That's his mermaid."

"But there's no signature." Colby walked over to the small mermaid painted in the sea. It looked like the statue in the town gardens. "How do you know?"

She stared at him. "You're not into the whole town gossip thing, are you?"

"I try to stay out of it," he said.

"My sister is Jacob's daughter." She said this as though he were some kind of imbecile. "That mural is worth thousands."

He laughed. "Thousands? A mural?"

She crossed her arms and smiled back at him, but she still had that face that said she thought he was the stupidest person in the world. "Yes."

"Thousands?" He made a small huff, but he did hear about the big auction that had taken place during the festival. He stepped back, looking at what was left of the painting.

"If you get it professionally restored, you could get even more." She looked at the mural with complete awe, and suddenly he became hyperaware of her. And how good she smelled.

"Are you drinking?" he asked, looking back at the bottle sitting on the floor.

Her forehead wrinkled as though he was acting crazy. "I texted your dad this afternoon."

He stared back at her, waiting to hear why she was drinking their wine. "And that made it okay to take our wine?"

"I tried driving home, but I didn't feel safe in the snow, so I asked your dad if I could keep the car here for the night and clean for a little bit," she said, crossing her arms. "And it's my wine that I bought." She started to back up from him. "I should go home."

She marched straight to the bottle and picked it up off the floor.

He cringed at his earlier comment. "Look, I'm sorry. I didn't mean to sound so rude."

"I think you did," she snapped back at him.

He went to argue but realized he had come in hot and ready for a fight. "I'm sorry."

He looked down at her notebook and the drawing. Rectangles represented the store and the inside floor plan, along with its shelves and refrigerators. She had everything labeled and organized.

"Are these your sketches of the store?" he asked, pointing to the drawings.

She didn't say anything, just grabbed her coat. He reached out to give back the notebook and took a good look at her face, noticing it was puffy and red.

"Are you okay?" he asked, realizing she had been more than just upset with him. Something else was bothering her.

She looked at him. "I'm fine."

"Uh-oh," he said.

"What?" Her chest puffed out in defense.

"I know what fine means..." he said, turning back to the door.

"That I'm fine." She put the bottle onto the counter by the cash register, then went over to pick up the bucket in the corner of the room where he'd found her.

"That's really a Jacob O'Neill?" he said.

She stopped, the bucket's water sloshing around inside. "It's one the most magnificent pieces I've seen yet."

He almost rolled his eyes, but he remembered he had already been rude tonight. Sometimes this woman was just too much. Why did Ms. Boston need a job anyway?

Then he thought back to the credit card debacle that had caused his father to be even more sympathetic to the newcomer. She had probably maxed them out and needed some extra cash. She drove an Audi, for goodness' sake.

He took a step back and took in the whole mural. It ran almost the length of the side wall and reached the tall ceilings. A fisherman stood on the docks, unloading his catch for the day, the perfect, calm seas painted behind him. On the right side of the painting sat the town of Blueberry Bay and its valleys that rolled into the ocean.

"He must've been young," she said.

He tilted his head. "Is he the fisherman?"

She shook her head. "He painted blue sunny skies, but the

mermaid is there..." She walked over to where the small mermaid swam in the water. "That means he had a thing for mermaids before the whole storm."

"Right." Colby stepped closer and recognized the significance of the piece. Crazy Old Man Jacob hadn't lost his mind yet. "Before the storm."

"Do you want a ride home?" he offered.

She frowned, almost as though she were disappointed. "If you don't mind, I need to finish what I started." Then she added, "You don't need to pay me."

Figures. She was doing this for fun.

He hesitated before saying, "Sure. Why not?"

She went right back to the bucket, dropped a rag into the sudsy water, and then resumed cleaning.

"Why do you carry so much cocktail sauce?" she asked. "Do people really use this much?"

He closed his eyes, reminding himself that she was doing him a favor. "You know, you really don't have to do this."

She wrinkled her forehead. "You were complaining about it this morning."

"I did?"

She stared at him with that look, like he didn't have all the lightbulbs on. "Yes, you complained about how everything was so disorganized."

Ah, he remembered. "Yes, I did."

She lifted her eyebrows, seemingly saying *I told you so*, and went back to wiping off bottles of cocktail sauce.

"How's the baby?" she asked. "Healthy? Everything went okay?"

He didn't know why, but he felt a heaviness with the question. "She's perfect."

Remy smiled, then stared off, going so far away inside her head that he wasn't sure if she even remembered he was standing behind her.

"I can help," he said, not really wanting to but also feeling a bit guilty that she was doing something he had complained about.

The crease between her eyebrows deepened. "I'm good."

"Okay..." Was she telling him what to do? "What about that shelf?"

He pointed to the shelf that had been moved to a different spot.

She stood up, the rag dripping from her hands into the bucket below. "I've already done it."

Colby looked around the room, noticing all the shelves had been moved and the items cleaned and rearranged. Inside of the big, open space where the old refrigerators used to go were lines of shelves.

"If you put all the shelves together over there, away from the windows," she said, pointing at the shelves' new location, "more natural light will come in and you can showcase this mural. Plus, now people can move around the space."

He almost let out a chuckle. Who would actually come to a lobster market to see a mural? But by the way she stood there, staring at the painting, the more he thought she believed it.

He'd just move the shelving back later. Thank goodness it wasn't their busy season. And in the end, she'd done him a favor. He did want to organize those shelves.

"I put the shelves on that side—"

"For the Van Gogh?" Just as the sarcastic remark left his lips, her face flashed a look of anger.

Her mouth opened as if to say something back, but the anger faded into another look, and he felt immediately ashamed. Remy's eyes slanted down and away. Her arms dropped to her sides; her shoulders slumped. She dropped the rag into the bucket, and it plopped into the water.

"I'm good," she said, walking toward her things, leaving cleaning supplies on the floor and her bottle of wine on the counter. She stuffed her arms into her coat, then shoved her hands into her gloves. With a hard tug, she put her hat on and threw her scarf around her neck.

Just as Remy marched away, Colby apologized. "I'm sorry."

And that's when the worst thing happened. A tear fell down Remy's face.

"Yeah, well, I'm fine."

She left after that, slamming the front door.

He noticed her fashionable boots when she walked out to her car and groaned to himself.

"Just let her go, Colby," he said out loud as she jumped over a snowbank and into the empty street. Snow fell at a steady pace, and even with extra plows out that night, they couldn't keep up. She didn't go to her car but began to walk.

Best case, she'd get frost bitten.

Worst case, she'd get hyperthermia, and who knew what could happen.

He looked at the bottle of wine sitting on the counter. She'd had about half, which could make her feel warm enough.

"Ugh." He grabbed his coat and walked out of the store. He powered the starter and his truck hummed to life.

"I'll take you home!" he shouted out to her, but she didn't turn around. "Remy! Let me take you home!"

But she stomped through the snow and down the street. He rolled his eyes. He'd follow her home if he had to.

"Come on!" he yelled. "You're not going to be able to walk all the way."

He knew where she lived, and it was at least three miles from town, having to go all the way around the bay to the other side. She didn't listen, just soldiered on as though she couldn't hear him.

With the waves pounding off in the distance, maybe she couldn't.

He ran down the road to make sure. Just as he reached her, she whipped around and said, "Leave me alone."

Remy's face glistened with tears under the streetlights. Tears welled up in her eyes and wobbled on her lids. She looked away, up at the sky, wiping the back of her hands against her cheeks, and shook her head.

"I'm not crying because of you," she said as he stood there, dumbstruck on what to say. "This has nothing to do with you."

Suddenly, everything went silent. All he could hear was his breath and the pitter-patter of the snowflakes falling on his hood.

"Well, let me apologize for my part in it," he said. "I was taking out my own frustrations on you and I apologize. You helped me with Sadie, and I should have been kinder. Let me take you home."

She inhaled a deep breath and shakily blew it out. She looked down at her phone. "Fine."

If Colby thought it was cold outside, Remy's reception inside his truck was colder. Remy didn't speak the whole—very slow—drive back to her place.

When he arrived, the snow crunched underneath his tires as he pulled up. She opened the door immediately and jumped out. She quickly said, "Thank you," but didn't look back as she slammed the door and walked inside the house.

CHAPTER 7

*R*emy jolted up in bed for three reasons. First, Joe had sent a text that dinged her awake. Second, she remembered she quit her job in a drunken voicemail. And third, she had left her very personal notebook at the market.

Joe had sent multiple texts, and she couldn't read them without opening all of them, but she wasn't sure if she wanted to read what he had to say. Joe didn't usually even write texts. It was too slow. He wanted to talk quickly and get the conversation over with while doing something else.

She felt dread instead of relief while staring at her phone, wondering what the rest of his message said. It wasn't that something was off—everything was off. He'd written her name, which he never did. He usually went right to it. He would ask, *Why stop and type salutations when it was a direct message on her phone?* Same theory with signing or saying goodbyes or any irrelevant banter like *I love you* or *Miss you*. She should just know he did whether he ever said it or not.

She sat up further in bed, adjusting her pillows, wishing she hadn't had that last glass of wine last night, but she took a deep breath and opened the text.

Like a puzzle she couldn't decipher, she stared at the words.

They muddled together and she couldn't understand what he was saying.

He was mad. He wrote short and cold, even for her few-worded husband.

Remy. Enough. Come home.

I want to work things out.

It doesn't have to be this way.

Three separate texts. Three separate thoughts. Did he send the first and think about it? Then send a second to counter the first, then a third to counter the second?

But those three texts said it all.

He wasn't willing to change.

At all.

He continued to hold his power over her, and she was done with having him control her and her life. What Joe never understood was that the money, his power, wasn't what had drawn her to him.

The kind man who had given to the poor, helped his community, loved his family, that was the man she loved.

But that Joe hadn't been around in a very long time. And now, looking at that string of texts, she wasn't sure *that* Joe was even the real Joe.

Certainly, no Gordon or Jacob.

Her mother had two great loves in her life, two devoted daughters, and a career that had fulfilled her.

And what did Remy have?

Fourteen cents, a job that was in question—considering her performance last night—and she was living on her family's goodwill.

She was the definition of loser.

She threw her phone, which she couldn't afford, onto the bed, pulled the covers over her head, and closed her eyes. She would ignore the fact that she was supposed to help open the store. Or the fact that she had rearranged the store without permission in her emotional fit last night. Why did it hurt so badly that this wonderful family was blessed with a new baby?

But the fact that even scumbag Phillip, Meredith's ex, had been able to have another child killed her. He'd probably have a whole brood if he continued the way he was going. Remy's mother had joked that she hadn't even "tried" to get pregnant. Meredith had "looked" at Phillip and gotten pregnant with her three healthy babies.

And then there was Remy.

She heard a knock.

"Remy?" Meredith said through the door.

She squeezed her eyes, letting the tears fall onto her comforter. With a chipper voice, she said, "Yup?"

"Are you going to work?" her sister asked.

"No," Remy said, staring at the wall, waiting for the door to open. Meredith wouldn't care if she didn't invite her in.

"What?" Meredith said, knocking again.

Remy heard the doorknob twist.

"Are you not feeling well?" Meredith asked, coming into the room, instantly turning back into the big, over-protective sister. "What's wrong?"

"My life," she said, not moving.

Meredith sat down on the bed. "Want to talk about it?"

"Not really," Remy said. There was too much to talk about. Where did she start?

"So, you don't have work?" Meredith thought Remy had to work because that was what Remy had used as an excuse to go to bed when she'd gotten home last night.

Should she lie and just say she was going to work, then hide out in her car? Deal with it another day? Or did she just tell Meredith how she'd hit rock bottom and was drowning?

Then the sudden realization that her car was still at the market hit her.

She was too ashamed about her behavior last night to go back and grovel for her job. Even if Colby had been a jerk, looking back now through a clearer head made her flush in shame.

Why did she quit by leaving a stupid voicemail? What was she thinking last night when she called their machine?

She would be the talk of the town in no time; the strange sister of Jacob O'Neill's daughter.

"Did they close because of the power outages?" Meredith asked.

Remy looked up. She hadn't heard the waves. The storm must have blown through and was now over. She looked out the window. The sun rose to a blue sky.

"Is there a lot of snow?" Remy asked, sitting up in bed and seeing the ocean calm for the first time in months.

"There's a ton of snow," Meredith said, pointing out the dormer window that looked out at the front yard on the other side of the room. "And it's supposed to be forty and rainy tomorrow."

Meredith beamed at this, but Remy hated the winter, especially a New England winter. Cold, wet, and gray. The worst of all things in Remy's mind. She wanted something tropical— sunny, hot, and dry. Not that she didn't love Blueberry Bay, but winter in Maine started when most places just started feeling the fall weather.

"Do you think they're closed?" Remy asked.

"The whole town is," Meredith said. "The heavy snow brought down half the power lines." She smiled, patting Remy on the arm. "Remember when we were kids and we didn't have power?"

"And we'd make cookies in the woodstove." But Remy didn't have time to go down memory lane. She looked at the time. The clock flashed twelve o'clock. The market had probably lost their voicemails if the power had gone out. She might have a job after all.

That's when she remembered her car was parked in the loading zone.

"Do you think you could take me to my car?" Remy asked.

Meredith wrinkled her brow. "I doubt the roads are plowed."

"I'll have to walk," Remy said.

"It's a few miles, at least." Meredith stood up, checking outside.

"Yes, but I could use the exercise." Remy hadn't gone running or biking or swimming in weeks, or was it months now?

"Can I borrow your boots?" Remy asked.

Meredith looked at her. "Are you okay?"

"I'm just tired," Remy said. "Late night." But she avoided Meredith's eyes when she said it. Remy felt anything other than okay.

She sprung up, remembering the painting. How had she forgotten to tell Meredith last night?

Because her sister had been busy cuddling in Quinn's arms, watching a movie.

"There's a painting done by Jacob at the market," Remy said. "A mural."

"Really?" Meredith looked surprised. "I hadn't heard about a mural."

"It was covered by shelves of cocktail sauce." The thought killed her. "It's a landscape of the town from the point of view of the water. Not like his usual stuff. It's quaint, New Englandy, and before the accident."

"How do you know it was Jacob's?" Meredith asked.

"It had his signature mermaid," Remy said.

"Oh, wow." Meredith looked excited. "Let's ask Quinn to drive us. He has four-wheel drive."

Remy shook her head. "No, no, that's okay. Let me walk and I'll call you guys."

But Meredith was already texting on her phone. "Quinn said he never knew!"

Remy wished she hadn't said anything. Now everyone will know that she was crazy if they all head to the market.

"I'm really okay to walk," Remy said, but knew it was futile.

Meredith texted away on her phone. Could Remy blame her sister, wanting to see her father's painting? "Okay, let's go."

Remy got dressed and skipped breakfast, pouring herself a large black coffee instead. Gordon was already out when they met Quinn in the driveway to take them to the market.

With the full sun as high as it was, droplets of snow melted from the trees. Meredith greeted Quinn with a hug and a soft kiss, and Remy wondered if she should run to the store. She dreaded the idea of going back there. What would she say? Why had she told Meredith about the mural?

"When do you think Jacob painted the mural?" Quinn asked, immediately interested.

That's how Remy knew Quinn was the one for her sister. He was interested in everything about Meredith. He gave her his full attention—nothing seemed too frivolous or futile or foolish. He listened to her and never questioned her. Everything she said and did, he accepted and trusted.

Remy realized with a stabbing realization that she had never known that.

Joe had been fifteen years her senior and had acted like it. At first, she'd seen it as confidence. He chose the restaurants, the dates, the people they included. He frequently would tell her no, which she thought was his assertion, until he began saying no to her family.

He didn't like her mom "stopping in" at the house. He didn't like her brother-in-law, Phillip— she didn't much like him either, but since he didn't really like Phillip, Meredith also got cut out of the parties and gatherings they had a lot of the time, unless it was a holiday or her birthday. Joe wouldn't even include them in his birthday. But the final straw had been when her nieces and nephew had been cut from their yearly summer invitation to their Cape Cod house.

"What do you mean I can't invite my family to my house?" Remy didn't think she could get any angrier at that point in the argument, until Joe had begun to speak.

"*My* house," he corrected her. "I'm the one who earns *your* lifestyle."

Her heart had started pumping rapidly, and her ears had begun ringing. She'd looked down at everything she was wearing as he stared at her with daggers in his eyes. From the Louis Vuitton shoes to the six-carat diamonds she wore in her ears, all of it had come from Joe. None of it was hers.

Joe was a deal broker, owning one of the biggest financial firms on the east coast. She decorated friends' houses and spent her own money doing so half of the time.

Joe had been right.

So, she had applied for an interior design course at a local college.

"I want to design comforting spaces," she'd said one night at dinner.

"Comforting spaces?" he answered, his eyes on the phone.

"Yes, like hospitals," she'd said. She had thought of the room where she'd lost her baby boy, Matthew. It had been like every typical hospital. The colors bland and cold. The furniture hard and plastic. The commercial-print photos emotionless. Who wanted to lose a loved one in a room that looked like a cafeteria?

"I think the last place people care about decorating is hospitals," he'd said dismissively.

But the idea had kept rolling around in her head. Interior design was important whether her husband believed in her or not.

Even her professor had thought so.

"That's a really powerful way to comfort a patient," he had said to her after she'd turned in her project. "And your husband is Joe Moretti? Maybe you should talk to someone who knows someone. You don't need a license to work in interior design in Massachusetts. You have a natural gift with space and mood. Take that art degree you have from the University and get out there."

The implication had been that her husband could open all the doors for her. All she had to do was share her talents, and things would begin to happen for her.

"I'm not going to investors with this idea," he'd said after she had shared it with him.

"My professor said this was a solid idea. That people would really be interested in it," she'd said, taking back her computer with the slides she had created.

"Look, I know you don't understand my job, but I don't have time to talk to people about decorating a hospital." He'd pecked her on the cheek before walking away without hearing her response. "Don't forget we're having cocktails with the McGregors tonight."

She had listened to his footsteps as his wooden-soled leather shoes had hit the marble floor in the front hall and the door had slammed behind him.

She had decided to leave him then. She'd packed up her car with the things she knew had been hers and was ready to go, but she had chickened out when the caterers arrived at the house. As she stood at the party listening to Joe sell his usual lines to the new trending friend of the season, she did not want to be part of that life anymore—the fancy friends that came and went, the posh parties that were really to show off, and all of the fakeness that surrounded them.

"Are you coming?" Meredith asked her from the front of Quinn's truck.

Remy realized she had drifted off into her own thoughts and they had already arrived at the market.

"We're already here?" Her stomach sank as she opened her door. "Maybe they're closed."

Inside the market, all the lights were off.

Meredith jumped over a big snowbank. At the foot of the bank was a slushy puddle that Remy realized she was stepping in. Her boots were ruined.

"I see someone inside!" Meredith said.

"It's Colby." Quinn waved at Colby from where he stood on the sidewalk.

Remy saw that her car had been completely cleaned off and someone had plowed her out. She followed behind her sister and Quinn as they walked into the market, and what she noticed right away surprised her.

The store was set up just like her drawings.

She stepped farther into the store and saw everything had been put on the shelves and placed in order like she had doodled in her notebook.

Her notebook!

She looked over to her station and saw it closed by the register.

"Good morning," Colby said, looking right at her.

She immediately blushed. Did he know about her drunken voicemail? Was he still carrying a weird vibe like he had the other night?

"I heard congratulations are in store!" Quinn said, smacking Colby on the shoulder. "That's great news about Bridgette and the baby."

Remy's heart ached a familiar pain each time babies were brought up.

"Yes, it's very exciting," Colby said.

He turned to Remy and gave her a smile, but she didn't meet his eyes. She couldn't look at him with pure shame running through her. What had she said on the voicemail exactly? She couldn't really remember.

She promised herself from this point on, she wouldn't drink wine anymore unless she was celebrating life.

"Remy! My treasure hunter!" Emil said, coming from the back. "Did your sister show you Jacob's painting?"

"We just got here," Meredith said, warmly greeting everyone.

Emil ushered them toward the wall where the mural had been painted.

"What do you think?" Emil held out his arms. "Look at the painting!"

"Mural," Remy corrected.

With the morning sunlight pouring into the market, the painting looked even more stunning than before. The paint had chipped and faded from time, and there were nicks and damaged parts of the wall that had changed the integrity of the mural, but it could be brought back to its original glory with a restoration.

Meredith covered her mouth with her hand, and tears sprung to her eyes. Remy couldn't help but smile at her sister's reaction.

"I love this," Meredith said, pulling out her camera. "Have you told Greg?"

Remy hadn't. "I wanted to show you first."

Meredith stepped back and Remy noticed how her whole body slipped into Quinn's stance, like her body molded into him.

"Can you believe it?" Meredith asked Quinn.

He shook his head. "It's amazing."

It really is, Remy thought to herself.

"We should call the newspaper," Emil said.

Remy thought the same thing but didn't want to be pushy since she had quit the night before.

"You definitely deserve a raise!" Emil said, patting her on the back.

Remy felt like she was in the Twilight Zone but took it as a sign that the voicemail had been somehow lost. She finally caught a break.

Remy watched Meredith admire her birth father's art then turned around to look at the shelves.

"I removed them all but half a dozen," Colby said to her from behind.

She jumped a bit, not realizing he stood so close. She had been avoiding him after all.

"Excuse me?" she said, wishing she could read his mind. Did he listen to the voicemail?

"The cocktail sauce," he said, leaning closer.

She noticed all the boxes of canned goods were gone as well and wooden crates were piled against the farthest wall.

"You had some really good ideas," he said. The others moved closer to the painting, leaving Colby and her. "I came in early to make sure I saw you and apologize for my behavior last night."

The comment made her do a double take. *He* wanted to apologize?

"I'm sorry I was rude," he said. "Do you think we can start fresh?"

She nodded, second-guessing the Twilight Zone scenario after this kind apology from Mr. Grouchy. "I'm sorry, too. I shouldn't have rearranged everything without permission."

He shrugged his shoulders. "Well, it turns out you were right about the cocktail sauce and a lot of other things, too."

"The place looks great," Quinn said, walking over to Remy and Colby. "Did you remodel?"

Emil shook his head. "This was all Remy's idea." The older man held out his arms at the shelves. "My granddaughter said I should make a video for some app."

"Sadie told you to put the painting on the website," Colby said.

"That's not a bad idea," Remy said, thinking about all those of high society who'd love to see an original mural painted by the reticent Jacob O'Neill. "You'll get a lot of clientele just for that."

"To see a mural?" Colby shook his head as if he couldn't believe it. "I guess it's worth a shot."

Remy could feel the fight in her. She wanted to shoot back at him for not believing her. Didn't art bring in thousands, if not more, for this town? How many people had stayed and eaten around town for Jacob's auction alone? How many had come because of the beautiful landscapes he had painted that they'd wanted to see with their own eyes? This town was indebted to Jacob, and yet this guy who fished for lobsters questioned his worth?

"You're really good at seeing things," Colby said. "I'm even thinking about putting the counter by the door."

She blinked a few times, making sure he wasn't being sarcastic and she was correctly interpreting a kind comment.

"I mean it," he said, as if he'd read her mind. "I think you're right, even about the other items."

"You read my notebook?" She thought about all the other things she'd written in that notebook. All the stupid junk about Joe.

Colby shook his head. "I just flipped through the top pages, where you had the store stuff. The stuff you made me look at last night." He reminded her.

She looked at his eyes, trying tell if he was lying. Joe never had a tell. But Colby had either told the truth, or like her ex, he was really good at lying.

"Do you think you could help me set up the rest of the place the way you drew it?" Colby asked, waving at the empty space in the center of the store. "You said we should use kitchen tables?"

She nodded. "Farm tables."

"Old farm tables?" he asked like she was crazy. "I have a couple of portable plastic ones in the back."

She shook her head a little too violently, which made Colby's eyes widen. She held up her hands, trying to help her point, stretching out the space. "You want the vibe to continue from the painting to the floors to the tables to the entrance."

"And what's that vibe?" he asked, looking at her like she had a lobster head.

"Rustic Down East comfort. You want people to know that this is where they'll find the freshest seafood from a family that loves sharing their catch. A place where locals sell their goods that are homemade. A place that feels more like a family home than a business."

"I can't believe Jacob painted all of that," Meredith said. The size of the mural was a lot larger compared to Jacob's other work. He had never created something so large that they knew about.

But what else had Jacob created they didn't know about? "Do you know if it was commissioned, or if Jacob just painted it?"

Emil shook his head. "I know Jacob fished and probably sold his catch here like all the others in town, but no, I don't know. I had no idea the painter had even been Jacob."

"Do you mind if I take some pictures?" Meredith asked. "I want to send some to my children."

"No, please do," Emil said.

Remy walked around the counter and picked up her journal, hoping Colby wasn't lying, because every fear, hope, and secret had been written in that notebook. She lifted the front cover, checking the inside as if that would somehow tell her the truth, but she put it in her purse before she forgot it again.

She didn't want anyone else to read what she'd written inside that notebook.

CHAPTER 8

*C*olby didn't mean to read inside her notebook, but she had been the one who had pointed it out, told him to check out her designs. So, he had.

When he'd gotten back to the store after dropping her off, he hadn't wanted to head back home, because all he could do was think about Brynn trying to talk to Sadie. Was she trying to get custody again? Was she clean or pretending to be?

Not that his parents weren't great grandparents, but how could his sister leave them with her responsibility? Her actions had changed everyone's lives, including his. He would be on the water if he didn't have to help with the store. This was his favorite kind of day to be out there. The calm after a spring storm was a beautiful thing to witness from the ocean. Unlike the land, where people were frantic over Mother Nature's gift, the sea absorbed it, welcomed its plentifulness, and continued on.

He loved being out on the water, being in the middle of nothing and near no one. No better place to clear one's head.

He looked over at Remy, wishing he had just told the truth when he'd seen her lift the cover of her notebook, checking to see if he had done any damage to it.

He should just go over there and tell her the truth. He'd

opened it to find the sketches and saw some of her writing on the other pages too. It had been his name that he had noticed. Then he had recognized the rant in her handwriting. He had read plenty of his sister's diaries to know the difference between a regular entry and a rant. Remy clearly hated him.

He didn't mean to read on, but he couldn't help himself when he saw his name, though he had immediately regretted it.

Colby thought I stole. He has no clue about my situation yet judges everything about me. Does he know what it's like to lose everything? Does he know what it's like to see blessings of life all around you when you are tortured with only death? Does he know what it's like to be so desperate to survive each day that you question if you can?

He had stopped reading after that.

He had wanted to apologize better, not in front of everyone, but he couldn't find a good opportunity. He wanted to tell her more about what he thought of her sketches of the store, but she was clearly avoiding him as the day continued. She didn't smile hardly all day, and to say he was worried about her was an understatement.

He pulled the cash bags from the day before out of the safe and decided to go to the bank.

"Hey, I took out a couple hundreds," Emil said to Colby. "For Remy."

Colby thought his father wanted to give her a raise, but a couple hundred dollars? "Really? What about a raise?"

"That too," he said. "But she needs some cash, I think."

Colby scrunched his eyebrows in question. "So you're giving her a couple hundred?"

"She asked to return her bottle of wine yesterday," Emil said in a whisper. "She said she was sort of strapped for cash."

Colby thought about the wine bottle he accused her of taking.

"She wanted to return it?" he asked, feeling like a complete jerk.

Emil cleared his throat as Colby saw Remy stick her head through the office doorway. "Hello, Remy."

"I'm going to take my lunch break," Remy said, jabbing her thumb behind her.

Colby stood up, immediately feeling guilty that they were talking about her and her situation. Had she heard them?

"Yeah, sure, sounds great," Colby said, rubbing his hands together.

The two men looked at Remy as she flashed a quick smile, then letting it drop as she stepped out.

His father turned back around, stretching out his neck. "I don't think she heard us."

Colby hoped not, but he couldn't tell. He couldn't read that woman.

"I was going to go back to my old place and clean up the driveway," Colby said. He would also check the barn and see if there were any tables. "Do you and mom have any extra dining room furniture?"

"If we do it would be in the attic," Emil answered. "Why?"

"Remy had an idea of bringing in local products to sell." Colby shrugged. "I can see what she's saying about using the space differently."

He didn't want to be a tourist market. He wanted to sell fish, but the truth was, their profits weren't like they used to be. The market had served its purpose for his family, but at what point did they just let it go? The world had changed. The town of Blueberry Bay had changed. People were more likely going to come to the market to see a painting than to get a lobster, and that was the sad truth.

"Can you believe how many people came to see the painting today?" Colby asked his father.

Emil nodded. "I'm almost out of product."

Colby sat up. "Already?"

"I sold most of the fish this morning," Emil said. Most of the town came by to see the paint—" His father stopped to correct himself. "*Mural.*"

Colby rolled his eyes. Remy was still a pain, but she was onto something. They weren't a market where someone would buy store-brand cocktail sauce and basic feminine products. It needed to be a market where people visiting Maine for the peace and tranquility Jacob had painted came to buy supplies to make their stay even more Down East.

She had listed slogans to be displayed—*Fresh Maine Chowdá* or *Lobster Bake*. In her sketches, she'd used the tables for fresh produce and other local items like blueberry baked goods and honey. She had underlined *Fresh Sandwiches, Salads,* and *Charcuterie Boards*. Then she had listed brands of wines he'd never heard of, but when he'd looked them up, they turned out to be from local wineries in the area.

He didn't know much about those types of companies that came in and revitalized a failing business, but her notebook had ideas that could very well rejuvenate the market and bring it back to life and maybe even sell some lobster.

"What do you think?" he asked his father again. Emil hadn't responded one way or another about the notebook and sketches. "Do you think we should go with her ideas?"

He hoped his father would give the go-ahead.

"What do you think?" Emil asked.

Colby noticed how tired his father looked these days. Everything Brynn put him and his mother through, raising Sadie, and helping with Bridgette and now her baby had not been easy. It had worn him down. There was no doubt Emil and Colby's mother needed to retire, but how could they afford to? And give Remy a raise? Not that she didn't deserve it, but they couldn't afford it.

"I think it's time we revamp the place," Colby said.

He couldn't sleep at all last night, not just because of Sadie but because he couldn't stop thinking about the possibilities that could come if they just pivoted like Remy had suggested. They could possibly make more of a profit. He could get his father to change things at the store and climb out of debt, or they would have to sell. There was no other way.

If they sold, well, then things would get even harder, he suspected, for everyone including him.

That's why he needed to focus on managing the store and helping with Sadie as much as possible.

He loved his sister, but addicts are selfish, whether it's a disease or not. Addicts only care about their next high. They don't deal with the damage they cause. They just keep seeking out that escape. Sometimes he wished he could be that selfish. Just run away and let everyone else deal with the problems.

"I think a little change would be good for the place," Colby said, noticing someone stepping into the market—the typical new clientele Remy was talking about.

A man in a fancy flannel that no true Maine man would be caught dead in and boots that only someone with a lot of money could afford. Colby watched as he walked up to Remy at the counter. She pointed to the rack of wine. He said something that made her smile, and then she went back to her notebook. Colby wondered what else she was dreaming up. He watched as the man strolled through the store, passing all the items and standing in front of the wine rack. Then he went to the fish as if it were an afterthought. The fish was now the last on the list for their customers. Why hadn't he noticed this before? Now he couldn't unsee the problems.

The man stood at the fish counter. Colby walked over.

"Can I get you anything?" Colby asked, wishing he didn't have to do this part, but they couldn't afford another employee.

The man shook his head. "I was hoping to pick up some fresh oysters."

Colby pulled out a tray of oysters he had purchased from a buddy that morning. "Have some right here."

"On a night like tonight?" Remy said from the counter. "You want something hearty, comforting."

This made the man smile and turn around to face her. "Hmm, like a chowder."

She nodded, pointing at the clams. "Such an easy soup, but nothing more comforting."

"Do you have a recipe?" the man asked.

Colby wasn't a mind reader, but the man was clearly flirting with her by the way he leaned over the counter to hear her answer and how he complimented her recommendation as she explained her simple clam chowder recipe.

"I'll take some clams," he said, not even bothering to turn to Colby.

When Colby handed them over, the man's attention was solely on Remy.

"You don't need to overpower it with spices," she warned him as he checked her out. "Just salt and pepper."

The man nodded, sticking around after she handed him the recipe.

"You live here?" he asked as if surprised. "In Blueberry Bay?"

She nodded. "I just moved here."

"With your husband?" he asked.

Colby laughed at that, and both of them turned to look at him, but he pretended to be looking at something else and not listening to this man trying to pick her up.

"No, just me," she said.

"Well, we have something in common," the man said.

She looked up at him, her eyebrows wrinkled in confusion. "What's that?"

Colby wondered that, too.

"I just moved to Blueberry Bay myself," he said, holding out his hand. "My name is Roland. Roland Foster."

Colby had heard about the newcomer to town—a man who'd built one of the big houses along the coast. It was a modern design that Colby thought stuck out like a sore thumb.

"Nice to meet you," she said.

"I happened to attend the auction of Jacob O'Neill this past summer. Didn't I see you there?" he asked. "When I heard about the mural, I had to come down right away."

"You were at the auction?" she asked, suddenly smiling. "I'm sorry, but the whole day was hectic. Did we meet?"

He shook his head, and her face looked relieved. "I happened to hear about it taking place from a friend. I wanted to pick something up for the house."

Colby had looked up the worth of some of Jacob O'Neill's paintings and couldn't believe the value people put on art. They were worth thousands.

"Did you purchase a painting?" she asked. She smiled widely now.

Roland nodded. "The Boat Along the Shore."

She stared at Roland, a gaze of admiration and respect. A look she never offered to Colby.

"I love that painting," Remy said.

Roland turned to the wall. "The mural is so different from his later works. You can really see how young and naïve he was then."

"Exactly."

Colby wanted to roll his eyes. Naïve? He could tell that by a mural of their town? Why had Jacob been naïve? Was it that he was a simpleton? A fisherman from a dinky harbor town who hadn't had enough class like those from the city?

"He was probably asked to paint it," Colby said, unimpressed by their theories. It would have been his grandfather who had commissioned it. The man had been as simple as they came. He would have wanted something to showcase the town and its history. The mural probably had nothing to do with Jacob O'Neill in reality. "Probably, just to sell fish."

"I don't think so." The man shook his finger but gave Remy a look. They had a silent understanding that Colby was an idiot.

"I hope you enjoy your soup," she said to him.

The man held up his bag, undeterred, and said, "I'm about to. Thanks for the tip."

She pointed toward the front of the store. "Stop by the farm at the end of Beach Plum Lane, and they'll sell you some fresh pota-toes and cream."

He opened the door. "Will do."

He walked out after that.

A bottle of wine sat on the counter. Remy swept it up with her hand and returned it to the shelf.

"He didn't want it?" Colby asked, waiting to hear about the quality.

She shook her head. Then in a sarcastic tone, she said, "He was going to look for a better brand at the grocery store."

She said this as if Colby should be embarrassed by this. He had wanted to ask her more of her thoughts about the sketches, but her condescending tone and snobbery was too much. Rome wasn't built in a day. He would ask her about those things another time.

CHAPTER 9

*R*emy stood behind the counter, waiting for the day to end. She was still slightly hungover, embarrassed, and tired. She was tired of not sleeping. She was tired of feeling sad. She was tired of feeling nothing one minute and then having all her emotions heightened at once, overwhelming her. She was so tired.

Now she was certain the handsome man named Roland had been flirting with her, but she'd had no energy to respond. Even if he was good looking and obviously had some money, Remy wanted nothing to do with men.

She wiped down the counter as she waited for more customers to come into the market.

"Hello!" a young girl's voice sang out as the bell hit the glass of the front door.

Emil brightened immediately as the young lady came walking into the store. "How was school?" He came out from behind the fish counter and gave her a big hug.

Remy's heart tugged at the sight.

"Good," said the young girl. "But I had to play dodgeball."

"They still play that?" Colby asked, coming out from the back. "I thought that had been canceled long ago."

The young girl, who Remy discerned was Sadie, shrugged her shoulders. "I got hit in the face of course, by stupid Dylan Hooser."

Sadie pointed to her cheek, which looked the same as the other cheek.

"I think you'll make it," Colby said.

Remy smiled at the young girl, and that was when she saw the gold charm bracelet dangling along her wrist.

"I like your bracelet," Remy said to her.

The young girl's grin grew. She held it up, letting it fall a bit down her arm, then shook it. It had three small charms hanging on it.

"It's my special bracelet," Sadie said, proud of it.

Remy couldn't help but smile. "It's very pretty, just like you."

Sadie's eyes widened at the comment. "Thank you!"

Then the young girl looked at her grandfather. "Is this the new woman Uncle Colby got all rattled about?"

"What did you say?" Colby said from the shelves.

"Well, that's what Auntie Bridgette said," she said, her attention on the dangling charms. She turned back to her grandfather and asked, "Have you seen baby Camden this afternoon?"

Remy cast her eyes away from the happy family. She didn't need to be the mother of a child to experience joy like this family. She picked up her notebook and flipped to the next clean page, then scribbled down some words—prickly, suffocated, clammy. She wiped her palms against the hip of her pants.

Remy drew the beginnings of a cat, imagining it as her family in a short time. Meredith and Quinn's relationship had been moving at a very steady pace. Having her sister in the guest room was sure to be a relationship hazard soon. Gordon had looked for a small condo in Florida by a golf course to stay in during the winter months. He'd offered for Remy to stay with him, but how long could she live off her sister and father and Joe?

Maybe that was why the divorce burned so much. None of the past fifteen years had been hers. Even the alimony, now in her bank account, wasn't really hers. Joe definitely didn't see it that way. Remy wanted something of her own. To build something of her own. She didn't want to work for anyone. Well, maybe Emil wasn't so bad, but she needed to figure things out because she didn't want to work for anybody.

She wanted to work for herself. Earn her own money. Buy her own house. Get as many cats as she wanted. Adopt or foster as many children as she could. She didn't need to have a baby herself. She would do whatever she could to give any child who needed a mother a home.

Remy started a list.

Number one, career.

If Remy wanted to start a family, she would need a place to live. And she wasn't going to be able to afford a any place if she continued to work as a cashier in a market. No, she needed a real job with an actual wage that could pay for rent, or enough where she could save for a down payment.

New number one, new job.

Afterward, maybe she could start thinking about a career, but until then, she would find something where a raise meant more than a dollar. A real job with benefits and insurance.

She grabbed the weekly community newsletter that sat by the counter and opened it up to the want ads. She scanned the categories until she found employment. A lot of services were being offered, but not a lot in the way of employment. There were restaurants looking for servers, more cashier positions, a mechanic, and a gas attendant.

The truth hit Remy like a bomb. She wouldn't be able to live in Blueberry Bay unless she lived off her sister or father. There was no other way. There were no other jobs. She'd have to go back to Boston.

That was when the bell hit off the door's glass and the customer from earlier stepped in.

"Did you forget something?" she asked, looking up from the newspaper.

Roland nodded. "I forgot to ask for your number."

Remy heard Sadie gasp from behind the fish counter and noticed Colby turned to see what his niece was reacting to.

Remy's face flushed as Roland stood there smiling at her.

Her first reaction was that this man had incredible confidence.

Her second—he reminded her of Joe.

She smiled back. "I'm happy to share more recipes if you'd like."

He laughed at her joke but didn't back off. "I'd love to have you to my home for chowder." He said it with a hard R. Not like a local, who'd drop the R altogether.

Remy shook her head. She had no business going to dinner with anyone. "Thanks, but I'm afraid I'm busy."

He laughed at this. "I haven't told you when."

Hadn't he? She swore he'd said tonight. She stopped listening because she didn't need to go on a date. She didn't even want to be around men, especially one who reminded her of Joe.

"I live over on the other side of the bay from your place," he said.

"My sister's place," she corrected him.

"That's not your cottage?" he asked.

And that's when she realized he thought she was the daughter of the late, great artist Jacob O'Neill.

"No, it's my sister's." She went back to the newspaper.

"I thought Greg said you live there too," he said.

The mention of Greg made her look up immediately. "You know Greg?"

He nodded. "I begged him for a seat at the auction."

She laughed at the coincidence. "You're kidding me. What a small world."

"I should've started off with that, I guess." He laughed at himself, shaking his head. "Hi, my name is Roland, and I think we have a mutual friend."

Her smile grew at his response. "Wow, that's really crazy."

How friendly was he with Greg? She could easily text him and get his rating, from psycho to perfect. Greg's rating for Quinn? Beyond perfect.

"So?" he asked again. "Dinner with a friend of a friend?"

She looked down at the six job openings. Did she just lay out her problems like the paper? "Thanks, but maybe another time."

Roland stuffed his hands into his pockets. His smile faded only slightly. "Would it be okay if I continue to shop in the market?"

This made her jerk her neck back. "Of course. I can't stop you from shopping."

"What if I just want to come and talk to you about how my chowder comes out?" he asked.

Her heart skipped a beat, and she didn't like it. She didn't like it one bit. "Um, sure. I'd like to hear how it goes."

He nodded, staring at her with his dark brown eyes. "Good to finally meet you, Remy."

Remy stared back, unable to look away, but she could feel her emotions stirring, like a bottle of water being swirled around. "Yes, good to meet you, too."

CHAPTER 10

*G*inny Michaud slammed down the gavel, with its blueberry shaped head, on the front table. "It's time, ladies…and Quinn."

All the Queen Bees sat on the second floor of the town hall and caught up before the first Queen Bee Gardening Club meeting of the year began. Joyous conversation filled the room, and even though the gavel fell multiple times, the ladies kept on talking.

"Alright, time to begin the meeting," Ginny said a bit louder.

All the ladies settled into their seats, quieting down.

"I told my doctor," Carolyn, the oldest Queen, said to Susan, who sat next to her, "if I'm still waking up every day, then let me have my cocktails!"

"Carolyn!" Ginny called out over her older sister. "We're starting."

Carolyn waved at another Queen coming in late, ignoring Ginny, then crossed her arms, sitting back in her chair. "When are you going to start, Ginny?"

Ginny rolled her eyes and hit the table again. "Alright, let's begin with the pledge."

The whole room stood up and turned to face the American Flag hanging next to Maine's state flag, and a homemade town flag made by Susan.

Remy began saying the words with her hand over her heart when an unexpected emotion of sadness washed over her. She may need to leave all this. Just as she was feeling like she was a part of things, she would have to leave. What would she do? Where would she go?

"Let's get right to it," Ginny said.

"When are we going to be able to start drinking at these things?" Carolyn said, cocktails still on her mind.

"You know we can't drink on city property," Ginny said, scowling at her sister. "Now, if we could please begin."

"When is the barn going to be ready so we can start drinking?" Carolyn said back to Ginny.

Ginny stared at her sister, her mouth ajar, clearly at a loss for words.

Meredith raised her hand. "As soon as the weather permits it. Quinn put in lights, so we can have our meetings there."

Carolyn and the ladies around her applauded at the news. "That's wonderful, Meredith!"

"I told you she should be the Queen for the festival!" Carolyn said so loudly the whole group could hear.

"Have you turned on your ears, Carolyn?" Ginny said to her sister.

Carolyn continued to talk to Susan, completely unaware of Ginny trying to get her attention.

"Turn on your hearing aids, Carolyn!" Susan tapped her ear with her finger.

Carolyn cupped her ears with her hands, and she adjusted her hearing aids.

"I'd like to start by thanking Meredith and her family for allowing us to continue to work in the fields this summer for the festival," Ginny said.

Everyone started clapping, including Remy. She could not be prouder of her sister. The year Meredith had gone through had been horrible. Her husband had divorced her out of nowhere, had a baby with a thirtysomething, and never seemed to care that he had destroyed her.

Tears glistened in her eyes thinking about breaking vows and cheating husbands. Feeling like a victim, like Meredith, would be completely wrong. From the outside, Joe was a devoted husband. Why would she think she'd change him and turn him into a family man just because he had married her?

"Let's start with new business," Ginny said to the group. "We need to send flowers to the St. Germains. Bridgette had her baby."

"I'm proud to announce my new grandbaby!" Lucy St. Germain shouted out to the group from one of the back seats. "Camden Carroll."

Remy turned around to get a better look. Carolyn clapped from the other side of the room, her hearing aids now fully turned up.

Remy had only met Lucy a handful of times. She didn't come down to the market very frequently like the men did. She had heard Emil joke to one of the regulars that she didn't like smelling like fish.

Oh, goodness, did Remy smell like fish now?

"She's a perfect five pounds, four ounces." Lucy beamed as she spoke.

The baby's size seemed a bit small, but Remy didn't know if that meant too small or just petite. She didn't know much when it came to that kind of thing. All she knew was the longing of wanting a baby and the aching of losing a baby, with nothing else in-between. It felt so unfair.

The meeting moved right along. The Queen Bees decided to hold their annual garden day party, which was a nicer name for yard work, next week, and Remy volunteered to help.

On the ride home, Remy turned to Ginny who sat with her in the back seat and asked, "What happened to the St. Germain's other daughter, Sadie's mother?"

Remy wasn't sure if she was crossing a line asking a personal question like that. Blueberry Bay had been welcoming to her and her family, but did they trust her with their secrets? Emil and Colby certainly didn't enlighten her about their situation when she bought feminine products for Sadie.

It truly wasn't her business, but there was a story there.

It was Quinn who answered. "Sadie's mother is an addict. Can't stay clean. Terribly sad situation."

Remy instantly felt ashamed she had asked. Addiction ruined so much. Remy thought about Colby and their interactions at the store since she had started working at the market. He reminded her of Meredith when she was running around after three children—always five minutes late, a million things that needed to be done right then, and never enough time to do anything. Short with everyone.

"Emil and Lucy are Sadie's legal guardians," Ginny continued. "But Colby's the one raising her. He moved back when Sadie was taken from her mother."

"The state had to take her away?" Remy asked.

Ginny shook her head. "Emil and Lucy fought for custody."

"But then Emil had the heart attack," Quinn said from the driver's seat. "And that's when Colby moved in."

Remy wondered where Sadie's father was, but she wouldn't ask.

How hard it must have been for the young girl. To lose her mother to addiction, a father that didn't take her, then to have your guardian and grandparent have a heart attack. That was too much for anyone.

"That poor girl," Meredith said.

Remy knew Meredith was thinking what she was thinking. Thank God for their mother, Jacqueline. Meredith's own father had suffered from addiction problems, which was the reason their mother had left him and taken Meredith away.

Remy couldn't help but feel a little bit differently about the ogre at the market. No wonder he was so grumpy.

When they got home, Gordon invited Ginny over for a nightcap with Meredith and Quinn. They all assumed Remy would join and not be a fifth wheel. Not that she minded being a fifth wheel, but their happiness, their security in their situations, made her situation tighten around her like fishing line digging into her skin. She had no security. Nothing.

"Are you headed to bed?" Meredith asked, but Remy could feel there was more to the question. Remy had been going to bed earlier and earlier.

"Yeah, just going to read," she said, climbing the stairs and feeling out of breath. "Good night."

"Good night!" They all sang to her, but a lively conversation started immediately after she disappeared up the stairwell.

Once in her room, she shut the door and kept the lights off. The night sky blended with magentas and oranges as the sun faded behind the inky black sea.

Was she truly a selfish person for wanting a child so badly? Was being a mother worth losing a husband?

She wished she had her mother to ask for help. She looked at the painting on the bedroom wall. Her mother must've painted it while still married to Jacob. Jacqueline's impressionist landscapes were her signature pieces. Soft, gentle strokes, but quick move-ments to show the moment as fluid and flowing. The waves' spray catapulting into the air. The pounding of the waves colliding against the granite ledges. The wind blowing against the water's surface and up the shore.

She wanted nothing more than to stand there with Jacqueline and ask her how she'd kept going. How had she painted such beauty when her husband had lost his mind? How had she painted such a serene landscape when so much of her life at that point had been destroyed by its waters? How had she moved on and kept painting the beauty and not the darkness like Jacob had?

Because everyone faces conflicts in their lives. There are two kinds of people.

There are people who see life as beautiful like Jacqueline and other people who are scarred by its darkness like Jacob.

CHAPTER 11

For the first time since spring, the morning had a warmth to it.

"Leave it to New England," Gordon said, opening up the back door.

"What's that?" Remy asked when he stepped out onto the back porch.

"If you don't like the weather here, just wait a minute." Gordon sipped his coffee, standing comfortably in just a fleece vest.

"Wow," Remy said, looking out at the water. "Look at all the ducks."

Dozens of black and white birds floated along the waves.

"I read that the long-tailed duck migrates at night," Gordon said, sitting down on the couch. "That's why they just suddenly show up."

Remy poured herself a cup of coffee and went out on the deck, taking off her winter coat. "It is nicer today."

"Nothing stays the same, especially the weather in New England," Gordon said, raising his mug to the sunrise.

Remy enjoyed mornings like this. It made thinking about a

new place to live that much harder. She enjoyed living with Gordon and Meredith. It felt like it had when they all lived together before, like they were just waiting for her mom to wake up. But everything changes.

"I think I'll walk to work today," she said.

"That sounds like a good idea," Gordon said. "Get some fresh air."

The constant wind of the Atlantic had calmed down to a slight breeze, so Remy decided to take the long way. She needed to think. No more sitting around feeling sorry for herself. When had she become such a wet rag, allowing life's challenges to bring her down?

So what? She couldn't carry children to full term. She could help some other child.

And she would give that child, whomever it was, a home.

A child that didn't have a mom.

Or a dad. Or an uncle.

She looked out at the vista creeping through the trees. Pines mixed with birches and blueberries. She could just make out the village of Blueberry Bay and the red market along the harbor's edge. Colby came to her thoughts. She wondered what he thought about having to pick up the pieces and raise this young girl. From what she could tell, the family had done a wonderful job with Sadie. She seemed like a happy, well-adjusted kid, but she knew nobody was perfect.

Maybe there was another Sadie out there who just needed someone to love her.

Remy had a lot of love. She was sure of that.

She needed to start looking for a full-time job. One with some benefits. She could manage something, run a store of some kind. She could apply to museums around the area. Her art history degree could be of some use…maybe?

She would apply to anything, get a second job, whatever it took.

She wanted to care for a child and someone who needed love.

She thought about texting Greg again. Maybe her college friend could help her. Pulling out her phone before she could change her mind, she texted, **Anyone looking for help at the gallery?**

Bubbles flashed on his end of the conversation.

You wouldn't believe it, but I was just talking about you.

She stopped walking, wondering why he was talking about her. When her phone started to ring, she expected it to be Greg, but instead an unknown number flashed across her screen.

Another text from Greg popped up as her phone rang. **I hope you don't mind, but I gave your number to my buddy, Roland!**

Her phone went to voicemail.

She dialed Greg's number right away. When he answered, she said, "What did you do?"

"I gave him your number," he said. "Thank me later."

"I don't want to date," she said, looking around the empty street to see if anyone had heard her.

"Okay, but you do want help, right?"

"With finding a job, not a guy."

"Roland is looking for an interior designer for his summer house up there," Greg said. "Remember, he's the one who lives in that contemporary on the other side of the bay."

The window house, she called it. The whole back end was nothing but windows. She knew those kinds of houses. The ones that tore down the fishing cottages or natural landscapes, maybe even the ancient blueberry bushes that had been growing along the Maine coastline for thousands of years. The ones who thought money and power trumped everything else, including family, traditions, and promises.

"Does he have a wife?" she asked, wondering if he was that kind of a guy. Take off the ring when a pretty woman was nearby.

"No, never married," he said.

"Oh," she said. She wasn't into forever bachelors. Not that she was into Roland, though he was very attractive and had great taste. The truth was, she wasn't into anyone.

"Listen," Greg said. "You need to get out. Forget about Joe and get that confidence back."

"It's not as easy as that," she said. It was much more complicated. And she tried not to get annoyed that one of her closest friends was making it seem like her high school boyfriend had just broken up with her. "I just left a marriage of fifteen years."

"Remy, it's me," he said. "The guy who knows you and knows you're making excuses."

Making excuses?

Remy inhaled a long breath, about to give it to Greg, when she listened to the birds singing. She hadn't heard birds singing over the waves in a long time, not since fall. Between the winter winds and the strong icy currents, the Atlantic took center stage when it came to sound.

Was she making excuses?

"I want to have a family," she said. "And I want to do that by fostering, I've decided. I just think there are kids out there whose mom one way or another can't care for them, and since I can't carry to full-term, then maybe I'm supposed to be a mom to a kid like that…"

She trailed off as she heard herself speak. What did she really know about kids? She was a forty-five-year-old who could shop really well and throw a fabulous party. She hadn't even babysat in years.

"Really, Remy?" he said.

"Yeah, am I crazy?" she asked, feeling completely doubtful all of a sudden.

"No, I think that's wonderful," Greg said.

And Remy could feel her lungs expand as a ray of sunlight poked through the trees. She hadn't said her idea out loud to anyone before and just realized how scared she felt about the whole thing.

It was now out in the universe.

Remy wanted to be a mom.

"I've got to go," she said to Greg. "But if it's really a job. Let Roland know I'll call him back."

So, she marched straight into the Blueberry Bay Café when she saw the help wanted sign.

"You wait tables before?" the owner, Lindy, asked.

"Back in college," Remy said, though it was a pizza joint that catered mostly to drunk frat boys.

"Well, my customers are like family, and I'm like their therapist," Lindy said. "Can you carry a conversation?"

"I love having conversations," Remy said. She was the queen of small talk. It was the one thing Joe had complimented her on more than anything else. She could wine and dine better than anyone. No one intimidated Remy. "I'm happy to gab with the guys."

"Well, they maybe don't gab so much as they do complain," Lindy said. "Complain about the weather, their arthritis and their joints, the Red Sox. But they're loyal and will tip well if they like you."

"Sounds great," Remy said. Better than sitting around doing nothing with her retired father, who really wanted to have alone time with his new *friend*. "I can start right away."

"Your shift will start at five AM," Lindy said, waiting for a reaction, but Remy had no problem.

"I'll be here right on time." Remy reached out her hand and shook Lindy's.

"Here's a menu." Lindy handed over a lamented sheet of paper. "Get to know it before tomorrow."

Remy held up the sticky sheet and nodded to Lindy. "I look forward to it."

As Remy headed to the market, something rippled in her belly, almost like excitement, but she was also scared and could feel her anxiety heighten.

She wasn't sure if she should just brush it off or let it grow inside her, because the last time she'd felt this, she had just learned she was about to become a mom.

By working this second shift, it was one step closer to getting her own place, another step closer to fostering a child, and maybe becoming someone's mom.

CHAPTER 12

*C*olby watched as Remy marched down Main Street like a woman on a mission. He looked down at his watch. She was over an hour early, which had become more usual than not since she had started.

"She's a stunning woman," his mother said as she came up from behind him.

Colby shook his head out of his thoughts. Unfortunately, he was thinking the same thing. "And also temperamental."

"If your husband did what her husband did, you'd be temperamental too," Lucy said.

"Good thing I don't have a husband," he said, curious. "What did the husband do?"

He didn't know much about Ms. Fancy Pants Remy but did recognize that one day she'd had a whopper of a wedding ring and then it was gone.

"He's Joe Moretti," his mother said, as though saying the name alone would be enough.

"Who's that?" he asked.

"As in Joe Moretti, CEO of Moretti Investments and Brokerage Firm." Lucy shook her head. "He's worth millions and he gave her nothing in their divorce. Makes you wonder how bad it was to go from riches to rags. Or in her case, Real Housewife to cashier."

"She lives on the ocean in a beautiful cottage," he said, not feeling sorry for the woman who drove a car that cost more than his annual earnings. "She's doing fine."

"She's living off her family," Lucy said.

He looked out the window as she walked into the small breakfast café across the street. Within a few minutes, she came out with an apron in one hand and a paper in the other. She walked across the street to the market.

Colby pretended not to be looking at her as she walked in, but now he wanted to know more.

"Are you working at Lindy's diner?" Emil asked as she walked in.

Both Lucy and Colby waited for her to answer.

Remy looked confused. "Is Blueberry Bay Café Lindy's diner?"

"Sorry, yes, Lindy owns the café." Emil's forehead creased. "Gee, I wish I could pay you more, but things around here are pretty tight."

Remy shook her head. "No, no, I need a second income if I'm going to stay here," she said. "I can't seem to find much in the way of art curators for galleries and such."

She was a curator?

"Did you work for a museum?" Emil asked.

She nodded. "I was a curator at a small gallery in Boston, but that was years ago." She turned to look at the mural. "Did you put a spotlight on the mural?"

Emil stuffed his hands into his apron's front pockets. "And I ordered a plaque to put beside it."

"You could even generate some news around it, like a grand showing," she said. "Put it in the paper. You should coincide it with the new spring season."

"That's an amazing idea," Lucy said, coming out from the

back. She went straight to Remy and kissed her on the cheek. "We could do it during the Blessing of the Fleet ceremony."

"The Blessing of the Fleet?" Remy asked. "I've never heard of it before."

Lucy clasped her hands together. "It's a wonderful tradition, especially considering Jacob's past. It's a time where the town celebrates our fishermen and blesses them a safe and prosperous season."

"That's beautiful!" Remy put her hands on her chest. "Do the Queens do anything with the blueberries?"

"Don't even get her started," Emil said. "They have a special event for everything, those Queens."

"We have a lobster dinner night where we auction off dinner dates!" Lucy said, wiggling her eyebrows up and down. "Lots of single men around these parts."

That was when he noticed Remy shoot a look over at him, her face going white, and she shook her head as though the idea of being on a date with Colby would be the worst possible thing.

"I'll have to watch out for that," she said, walking to the back.

He almost chickened out but grunted and grabbed the box he had put together from her notes for premade charcuterie boards. He walked to the back, where she hung her coat on a hook.

"Hey," he said, feeling like a complete idiot. "I made a sample of those board things."

"A charcuterie?" she said.

"Yeah, that." He handed over the box and immediately regretted it when he saw the look on her face. She thought it was as stupid as he felt. He went to grab it from her, but she pulled it back. "I'll just take it. I shouldn't have made—"

"It's a good start," she said, looking inside the box. He had put crackers, a port wine cheese, nuts, jellies, a full chunk of pepperoni, and olives in a box with lobsters decorated on it. "The lobsters are actually cute." She pointed at him. "You could do a basket with lobster essentials." She handed back the box. "But would you mind me showing you what I was thinking?"

99

He looked down at the box and could see the lack of something. Remy examined the box, giving constructive feedback that wasn't too judgmental. And he didn't know what it was about Remy, but she definitely knew what she was talking about. Ever since he had moved things around, other things that hadn't sold in years were now coming off the shelves. Besides, what did he have to lose? "Sure. Why not?"

That's when Remy smiled, a full, wide grin that made his stomach do a somersault.

Remy *was* stunning.

"So, what were you thinking should go inside?" he asked, when the bell to the front door chimed against the glass. He looked out to the front and saw Roland walking into the market holding a basket in his hands.

"Roland," she said, walking out onto the floor and leaving Colby mid-conversation. "What are you doing here?"

He held out the basket, the kind with a top, and opened it in front of her. "I made your soup and thought I'd bring you a sample."

Colby strained his neck to get a better look. Inside the basket was a loaf of bread, a container of what must've been the soup, and some other things he couldn't see.

"This is so nice of you," she said, pulling out a flower from inside. "I love daffodils."

"I heard you worked on a few interior design projects for Greg back in Boston," he said.

She nodded. "Yes, a few condos in the Back Bay area."

This fascinated Roland. "I've been looking for a decent interior designer since I built my house, but I haven't found anyone."

Colby rolled his eyes. It was clear this guy wasn't looking for anyone other than Remy.

"You have an eye for design," Roland said, but with so much cheese, Colby expected to hear Remy laugh like he wanted to, but she didn't.

"Thank you," she said. A wave of hope washed across her face, and it made something sink in the pit of his stomach. "Maybe I can come by and give you some advice."

"I'd love that." Roland placed the basket onto the counter, then pulled out his wallet from the breast of his blazer. "Here, take this."

Roland held up both hands once she took the small card.

"You don't have to call, and it's only for business, this number here." He pointed to the fine lines at the bottom. "But if you wouldn't mind just taking a look."

She flicked the corner with her thumb. "Maybe I can. I'd love to see inside the house of windows."

She knew where he lived?

And why did Colby care?

"Why don't you ask her out before he does?" Lucy asked from behind him.

Colby wrinkled his brow at his mother. "She's impossible."

"She's lovely," Lucy said. "She helped her sister with Jacob's cottage."

"She's not a saint just because she convinced her sister to keep a million-dollar piece of property," he said, still not understanding why the whole town was infatuated with her. "She's a know-it-all."

"Who knows what she's talking about," Emil said, looking through a catalog.

"What are you looking at?" Colby asked.

Emil passed over the glossy-paged booklet. "This is what they do in Boston."

Colby turned the pages, glancing through the professionally done photographs and designs of a high-end market.

"It looks more like a restaurant than a market," Emil pointed out. "Look at what they're carrying." He pointed to a small refrigerator. "There's only one counter."

Colby wanted to fish. Not sell charcuterie baskets with cheeses he couldn't pronounce but he couldn't ignore the figures they were earning over just the few changes Remy had made.

"This is what Remy says people are looking for here," Emil said, the same hope in his eyes he saw in Remy's when Roland said he wanted her advice on design.

"I think this place needs a change," Colby said, wishing he could afford to hire Remy. "What does Bridgette say about this?"

His little sister wanted the market to work just as much as Emil and Lucy did. Eventually, Colby hoped one of his siblings would want to take over, then he could get back out on the water again.

"It's risky investing in more products," Emil said to him. "But I agree. I think she's on to something."

That's the thing he was learning most about the woman—she was always right.

He looked back out at the front and noticed Remy talking to Roland.

Sadie suddenly appeared out of nowhere. "Nana's right. Why don't you ask her out, Uncle Colby?"

"Why aren't you in school?" Colby asked, suddenly not sure what day of the week it was.

"Remember I told you I have the day off for teacher workshops?" She spoke to him as if he were geriatric and losing his memory. She grabbed a spot next to him to look out the door that separated the back room to the floor of the market. "She's nice."

"She can be kind," he corrected his niece. Nice wasn't a word he'd use for the city girl, but she could show kindness when she felt like it.

"Looks like she's going to be asked out by that rich guy," Sadie said.

Colby watched as that rich guy made Remy laugh. The sound traveled all the way to the back, and like the wind, her voice struck him. He liked it.

He pushed open the swinging door and walked out to the front of the market.

"Looks great in here," Roland said loudly. "Much better set up than before."

"Yes," Remy said, looking around at the newly placed shelves. "It flows better."

Colby's jaw muscles tightened as they continued to banter about what was wrong with the market.

"When can you make it over to take a look?" Roland asked Remy.

"How does tomorrow morning sound?" he heard Remy ask, then held up his card. "I'll text you in the morning."

"That sounds wonderful," Roland said. "I'll see you tomorrow."

Colby watched as Roland left the building and headed to his large black overpriced SUV.

"This is more like I was talking about," Remy said from the counter as she opened the basket Roland had left.

"Excuse me?" Colby said, shaking out of his stare.

Inside the basket, a checkered gray-and-white cloth sat underneath small containers with oyster crackers, seasonings, a small salad with a container of dressing, and other fancy products Colby didn't see often enough to know exactly what they were. The whole display looked like something from the fancy Boston market magazine—steps above his box with nuts and pepperoni.

"If we were to start going in this kind of direction," he said, pointing to Roland Foster's basket. He waited for a smart remark in return, but instead Remy waited for him to finish. "Where would *you* start?"

"The Queens," she said.

"The gardening club?" He wasn't sure if she was being serious or not.

"Yes, they'll know a lot of the local farmers and wineries in the area." She said it as though it were obvious. "You want to sell fresh Maine products. Anyone can go to the grocery store, but not everyone can get to Blueberry Bay."

"Don't people want products they're familiar with?" he asked. That's what he had seen his whole life. Tourists came in and wanted the things they had at home.

"Not this kind of customer," Remy said. "They want to have the freshest, most unique experience. They're coming for the lobster they see on television. Most of them don't even know how to cook it."

That was true. He thought about it. "And carrying blueberry jam is going to sell more lobsters?"

"Yes," she said without hesitation. "They'll think about returning for lobsters when they're back home with that jam they bought that time in Blueberry Bay."

She sighed.

"The truth is, this building, the red market at the end of the harbor, is the reason why many people walk through the doors," she said. "But then you come in to nothing but fish that many are intimidated to cook and random household items."

He tried to take her constructive criticism with a grain of salt. He didn't need to get defensive, because as he listened to her precise details of what was wrong with the market, he agreed with everything she said.

"Do you have a list of vendors in the area?" He knew of some places but not specifics.

"Go to the next meeting," she said. "The Queens will give you all the information you need."

He hadn't ever thought about attending one of their meetings.

"You think they'll know suppliers?" Colby wasn't sure. These women were almost all retirees. What would they know about trending dinner art—as Remy referred to it—that goes with fish?

"Some suppliers?" she asked, rolling her eyes as she crossed her arms against her chest. "They'll know them all."

Colby looked out at the store floor. A few fishermen were talking to Emil about town gossip, not trying to sell their catch. The business would grind to a halt pretty soon if Colby didn't start figuring things out. Maybe this woman did know what she was talking about.

"Hey, Remy," Sadie said, coming out from the back.

"Hello, Sadie." Remy gave a warm smile. Then from her purse, she pulled out a small, wrapped gift. "I found this and thought you might like it for your bracelet."

Remy passed the gift to Sadie, whose face beamed with excitement. "Seriously?!"

Sadie ripped off the carefully folded and expensive-looking paper and threw it onto the counter in front of Remy.

"Did you paint this?" Sadie asked, her fingers brushing over a small mermaid painted on a white box the size of her palm.

Remy nodded. "It's the mermaid out in the park."

Colby had to close his mouth as Sadie opened the box and inside sat a gold mermaid charm.

"She's the goddess of the sea," Remy said.

"I love it!" Sadie immediately went to unclasp her bracelet from her wrist.

"Here, let me help," Remy said, taking Sadie's wrist into her hands. She gently removed the bracelet and handed it to Sadie, who put the charm on.

"Thank you so much, Remy!" Sadie ran around the counter and into Remy's arms.

Colby watched as the two embraced, both holding each other comfortably like they had been friends forever.

"That's very nice of you," Colby said once Sadie went to the back.

Remy shrugged. "My pleasure."

He wanted to ask why. The gold charm looked a lot more expensive than the bracelet he'd bought. Not that his had been cheap. It was way more than he would normally spend on that sort of thing, but he'd have spent twice as much to see Sadie's face when he gave it to her.

Remy knew what she was talking about.

"When's the next meeting?" he asked.

She looked up from rearranging the items on the display by the counter and smiled. "There's a meeting next week."

He nodded. "Okay. Then I shall see you there."

Her nose wrinkled at his phrase, and he wanted to smack himself in the forehead. When had he ever used the word, shall?

Then, like the mermaid statue, she smiled. "Then I shall see you there."

CHAPTER 13

*R*emy had started working at Blueberry Bay Café the day after she had applied. It turned out to be the perfect schedule. She woke up early, and Gordon drove her to work and had a cup of coffee along the counter with the other old men in Blueberry Bay. He'd go back to the cottage while she worked the morning shift, then she would head over to the market.

Even though the shift was a lot, waiting tables and being on her feet all morning, she loved it. She quickly learned the regulars and joined in with their good-natured teasing. Gordon fit right in with the fellas, talking about the Red Sox lineup that year or complaining about how much taxes continued to go up.

At the end of the day, after working her shifts at the market and the café, she was exhausted and slept like a baby. Coming home to Meredith and Quinn didn't sting so hard because she didn't feel as isolated as before. Taking part in everyday conversations made her feel like she was a part of things, like she was contributing.

"Your father tells me you paint like your mother did," Lindy said at the end of one of Remy's shifts. "Said you're quite talented."

"I did in college," she said, but she should've added that she hadn't done it much in years. "But he's also my father and loves me."

"I saw the mural over at the market," Lindy said.

"Oh, that's not my work," she corrected her.

"It's Jacob's," Lindy said back, who clearly already knew. Did she think what everyone else thought; that Remy was Jacob's daughter, too?

"I'm not Jacob's daughter," she said.

"But you are Jacqueline's." Lindy smiled, making it clear she knew that as well. "She worked here. Did you know that?"

Remy was shocked. "No." She shook her head, completely floored. "I didn't know."

"When she was married to Jacob, before the storm." Then she reached out her arm toward the back wall. "I always wanted to paint a mural along the wall here, too. A panoramic of the town with the café."

Remy tried to smile, but the project would be too much for someone like her. She wasn't a professional artist. She dabbled and had an art history degree.

"I'm sorry, but I've never painted a mural," she said. "And I'm not a true painter. It's just a hobby to me."

"I'm not looking for professional," Lindy said. "I'm looking for someone who loves this town to paint something for generations to come back and remember."

Remy looked at the wall again. "It would be cool to create an art destination."

Blueberry Bay had been known as an artsy, folksy area. The village had prided themselves for being home to Jacob and other artists. The town park had been designed to place sculptures made by local artists throughout its gardens. Maybe the little café could join in on the art.

"I love the idea, but I just do crafty things nowadays," Remy said. She hadn't picked up a paintbrush in forever. She couldn't even remember the last time. Then out of nowhere, she had grabbed one of Jacob's brushes and painted the mermaid for Sadie.

"I'll pay you," Lindy offered.

"You haven't even seen my work," Remy said, laughing at Lindy's eagerness.

Lindy put her hands on her hips. "I think it could really make this place look great."

"You totally should do it!" Sadie said from out of nowhere.

Remy swung around to see Sadie and Colby walking into the diner.

"Hey, Sadie! Don't you look pretty," Remy said to Sadie, who had her hair down and wore a pink shirt. "Hello, Colby."

"Don't I look pretty, too?" he joked, sitting down at the counter with Sadie.

Remy placed two menus down in front of them. She smiled, looking at the handsome fisherman. His blue eyes glowed underneath his dark eyelashes, and her cheeks instantly warmed. She quickly looked away.

"What if it looks like a third grader did it?" she asked Lindy. She could try, and if it turned out bad, she wouldn't charge her.

"I'm sure it'll look better than what I can do," Lindy said. "Do you think you'd try?"

"I'll think about it."

Before she could stop herself, she looked over at Colby and Sadie when she noticed he was staring back at her.

Oh boy. Could Colby tell she was semi-attracted to him? He had that rugged, Maine-man thing going for him. Colby was the opposite of Joe. Colby kept a trimmed beard, but Joe would never go a day without shaving, even when they were on vacation.

He always liked to tell people that when he had started earning real money, the kind of money people dream about, he'd hired an assistant who'd come to the house and shave him before going to work every day.

Remy had hated it. Every house, every day, someone was there. She never had a moment with Joe by herself. She always had to share him. Whether it was with his assistant or clients or his phone, Joe was always unavailable.

And he never left the house without being ready to meet with clients, because he hadn't become Joe Moretti by waiting for clients; he hunted for them, even when he went out with his wife. And image meant everything to him.

One time she'd gone to the grocery store in her workout clothes, and when he'd found out, he'd gotten angry with her.

"What if you were to run into one of my clients?" he'd asked.

"Then they'd know I had worked out," she'd said, not understanding.

"But you weren't. You were shopping."

"I was comfortable."

"Yeah," he'd said, scrunching up his nose like he did when he disapproved of one of her decisions. "And sloppy."

Being fifteen years younger hadn't been a problem in the beginning. He had seemed to respect her point of view, especially when it came to art or home décor. He'd taken in everything she had said and even bought pieces she had recommended at prices she couldn't fathom. He'd taken her to Paris on a whim on his private jet. Swept her off to Turks and Caicos on a chartered yacht. Driven her with the top down in his Porsche to his house in Cape Cod.

She should've kept her career going. Had she listened to her parents, she would've never married Joe and quit working at the museum.

Always on his phone, had been Jacqueline's complaint.

"Does he ever get off that thing?" she'd asked almost every time he was around the two of them, which at the end of her mother's life was never.

Gordon had admired his work ethic and had been happy with his results with his own retirement, but he'd never trusted him with his daughter.

She should've trusted the two people that loved her the most. Why hadn't she listened to her parents?

"I think I want to get the waffles," Sadie said, setting the menu down. "With strawberries."

"Not the infamous blueberries?" Remy said, teasing her.

Sadie shook her head, lifting her upper lip. "I'm not into blueberries."

"You're not into blueberries and you live in Blueberry Bay?" Remy wrote down Sadie's order. "Want a drink?"

"Chocolate milk, please," Sadie said.

"Regular milk if you're getting waffles with those sugary, syrupy strawberries," Colby said.

Sadie groaned. "I'm a woman now. I can order chocolate milk if I want to."

Colby closed his eyes. "Fine, get the chocolate milk."

"We have fresh strawberries," Remy said, not sure if that would help the sugar intake.

"Hmmm." Sadie picked up her phone. "Yum."

Remy turned to Colby, waiting to jot down what he wanted. "You ready?"

His eyebrows burrowed.

"I can come back," she said, wondering if he was one of those who acted like they needed time but really knew exactly what they wanted.

"No, no, I'll get the—"

"Remy!" a voice called out.

Remy turned around to see Roland walking into the diner. She thought she groaned silently, but when she also heard a groan come from Colby, she wasn't sure.

"Roland," she said, putting the order pad down. "Would you like a seat?"

She looked around the crowded diner. The small café didn't have a lot of seating, but she found a single stool a couple seats away from Colby and Sadie.

She pointed to the empty spot. "Go grab a spot and I'll take your order."

She pretended not to notice Roland's surprised face, and the shame started to build up. What must he think of her? That was when she heard Colby clear his throat.

"Right, what can I get you?" she asked.

He glanced quickly over at Roland, then back to her. "I'll take the lumberjack."

"Fitting." She pointed her pen at his flannel shirt.

Colby looked down as if he hadn't even noticed he looked like a lumberjack.

"How would you like your eggs?" she asked.

"Over easy," Colby said after taking a sip of his coffee. "With sausage, not bacon."

"Got it," she said. She tore off the slip and clipped it onto the service rack, then she grabbed a mug and walked to Roland.

"Coffee?" she asked as she set the mug down. After working in the diner for a few shifts, Remy figured ninety-five percent of her customers have a cup of coffee and enjoy being served one right away instead of waiting.

"Yes, please," he said, taking the menu, but a distressed look creased between his eyes. "I didn't know you also worked here."

She forced a bright smile and poured his coffee. "It's the best place to get all the village gossip."

He looked away, frowning, and Remy immediately became embarrassed. What had Greg told Roland about her situation? "I wish you would've called me back."

She could tell Colby and Sadie were listening from their seats. "Oh, I don't think I can do it. I'm not a licensed interior designer. I used to do it more for fun."

"Then, for fun, come by my place and see what you might do," Roland said.

"Sure, why not?" She tapped the pad with the end of her pen. Though her imposter syndrome was kicking in. She wasn't at all qualified. People just probably placated her because of who she was married to. "Do you know what you'd like?"

Roland grabbed a menu and looked it over, humming as he scanned the list of breakfast items.

"I'll take an oatmeal." He placed the menu back. "With real maple syrup."

"Oatmeal coming right up," she said, scribbling it down and ripping the sheet off. "I'll be back with that syrup."

Remy couldn't explain it, but the look on Roland's face made her feel embarrassed about her situation. Was he only asking her because of her situation, and he felt pity? The look on his face when he saw her as a waitress, not a customer, spoke a million words. Did Roland look at her like the rest of the world as Joe Moretti's ex-wife? Did he think she was a gold digger like the half of them? Or did he feel sorry for her because she was an idiot that was now broke like the other half?

She walked to the oatmeal, ladled out a spoonful, and filled a bowl.

When she set the bowl down in front of him, the look of sympathy on his face made her want to tell him she hadn't married Joe for his money.

"Oh, I forgot the maple syrup," she said, turning back to the kitchen to grab it.

"Remy," Roland said from his seat.

She turned around to see him holding a bottle of syrup. "The other waitress already brought some."

She smiled. "Great. Anything else?"

He picked up his spoon and pointed it at her. "Just a time that you're free."

She shook her head. "Really, I don't design interiors."

"Hogwash," Gordon said, walking over with his coat. "I'm headed out."

Gordon stood next to Roland, looking at him.

"Okay, see you later," Remy said, not offering the introduction she knew Gordon was waiting for.

"Roland." Roland held out his hand. "I'm a friend of Greg from college."

Gordon's face brightened at the connection. "Ah! Greg had been such a help with the girls."

This made Roland smile. "Yes, he's very helpful."

"Then you do know Remy's lying when she says she doesn't design interiors." Gordon looked at her. "She can do wonders with any space imaginable."

Remy smiled at her father. He was sweet, but just because she had helped design their family's kitchen years ago didn't mean she should design any room in Roland's house.

"So, what do you say?" Roland asked, waiting for her answer. "It's got to be better than waiting tables in a diner."

She was sure he didn't mean for it to sound rude, but she glanced around to see if Lindy had overheard, and it was Colby's eyes watching and disapproving. The man always had a scowl on his face, but he wasn't going to pay her the kind of money that Roland could. And even if Roland wasn't very perceptive of his surroundings, interior design for her *was* better than waiting tables. Waiting tables was hard. She enjoyed her fellow employees and Lindy. She loved socializing with the customers and meeting everyone in town. But she was on her feet all day long. The diner was small and crowded with customers, which felt cramped and overwhelming at times. She liked working with people, but she didn't like taking a perfectly fine meal back to the cook and explaining why Mr. Kane said it wasn't cooked right and losing a good tip. She didn't like the hours. She also wasn't a huge fan of having to answer to more people in her life. And the tips, though generous most of the time, still didn't cover the costs of living expenses for one woman.

"Sure, I'd love to see it," she said, giving a small smile. "Tell me where and when."

Roland grinned wide, and she could see how he probably rarely got a no. She'd call Greg tonight and make sure he understood she wasn't interested in dating.

Anyone.

"Great!" Roland gave a wink. "It's a great space."

"If it's anything like it seems from the outside, I'm sure it's beautiful," Remy said, pouring more coffee into Mrs. Bryant's mug.

"Since you haven't called me yet, here's my address," Roland said, taking out a pen from the inside of his coat pocket. He scribbled down his number on the paper placemat. "Would tomorrow afternoon work?"

Remy couldn't use work as an excuse since everyone around her would know she was lying. "Sure. I look forward to seeing your vision for the space."

Roland got up and dropped a twenty onto the counter. He hadn't put his spoon into the oatmeal. "Keep the change."

He didn't even have the bill. "Thanks."

Gordon waited until Roland left and said, "What made you hesitate?"

"What?" she asked, although her father knew her better than most people—out of those who were alive, anyway.

"You didn't want to take the job," he said, jerking his head toward where Roland had left.

"He knows Greg." Remy grabbed his uneaten oatmeal bowl and cutlery. "Which means he knows about my situation with Joe."

"So?"

"So, he feels sorry for me, just like you and everyone else in this town." Her throat started closing up. She didn't even know why she was getting emotional.

"This could be your lucky break," Gordon said. "Everyone needs one of those, no matter their situation."

She forced a smile, but the back of her eyes began to sting. "I took the gig, so can we drop it?"

Gordon's eyes widened at the comment. "Sure."

"Sorry," she said right away. She could feel she had hurt his feelings. "I'm just overwhelmed."

Gordon gave her a knowing nod.

"I'm really not trying to be a jerk," she said, feeling the sting now in her chest. If she lost it, the whole village would know about the hysterical waitress at Lindy's. She'd end up a local legend just like Jacob.

"I know," Gordon said. "How can I help?"

"You can't, Dad. I love you, but you can't." She didn't want to take anything from anyone anymore, especially not her father. He was retired. He just lost his wife. He deserved not to have to worry about his daughter.

"Maybe tonight we can watch that documentary you recommended." Gordon left a couple twenties on the table. Double what he owed.

Remy didn't know what documentary he was talking about. "Was it Meredith who recommended it?"

He held up a finger. "Yes, it was, now that I think about it. But we should all watch it together. I'll invite Ginny and Quinn, too."

She didn't want to seem ungrateful, but she just couldn't take another night of being the fifth wheel. "I've got plans."

This surprised Gordon as much as the lie had surprised her.

"You do?" Gordon scrunched his eyebrows together suspiciously.

"I do." She nodded, but she didn't give any more information because she had none.

"Did you let Meredith know? Because she said she'd cook dinner tonight." Gordon said this as if Meredith was cooking for them, but they all knew she didn't usually cook, which meant she was cooking for Quinn. The dinner would go on whether Remy was there or not.

"I'll make sure to let her know," Remy said, clearing Gordon's cup.

He smiled. "It sure is nice being with both my girls again."

She smiled back. She was glad her father had found happiness after losing her mother. She knew he had been devastated and had a hard time getting back into the swing of life without his partner of over forty years. Jacqueline had been the love of his life. And Remy didn't blame him for wanting to have someone to spend time with during his last stages of life. Why should he sit alone just because his daughter was alone?

"I'll catch up with Meredith between shifts," Remy said, but she'd bet a million bucks that Meredith didn't care one way or the other.

"Don't tell me you're also working at the market, too," Gordon asked. He shot a glance at Colby and Sadie. "Don't you want to rest?"

She shook her head. "No, I need to start saving for a down payment."

"Remy, don't be ridiculous. We can help you."

"I cannot have anyone else support me." She shook her head hard.

"Thanks, Remy!" Anita said, getting out of the booth. "Have a good weekend!"

"You, too!" Remy said back.

"Your sister doesn't mind you staying until you can get back on your feet," Gordon whispered, but being slightly hard of hearing, he spoke loud enough to catch Colby's attention. "You should take some time and figure out what to do next."

She needed to busy herself because otherwise she would lose herself. That she was sure of.

Remy grabbed the dishes and dumped them into the busboy's bin, ignoring Gordon. "I'll be back, Dad."

Remy didn't want to have this conversation, not with the tears fighting their way to the surface. She needed to get busy, wear her body out so she'd fall asleep instead of staring at the ceiling all night, worried about what she was going to do next.

As a little girl, she would have trouble falling asleep at night, letting worries take over her mind. She worried she wouldn't find a husband as good as her father. That Gordon was the only one out there that would love her. And sadly, she'd been right.

She knew it was silly that she worried about him getting serious with Ginny. Remy adored Ginny, but no matter how much she tried to get over it, Ginny just wasn't her mother. It was hard seeing him happy with another woman when she still hadn't even begun to grieve her Jacqueline.

She picked up Anita's tip—generous for a small plate of toast and coffee, but not enough to make a dent in a down payment for a house.

"Order up!" Danny, the cook, yelled out through the window.

Remy saw it was Colby's order and grabbed the two plates.

After carefully setting them down in front of him and Sadie, she refilled his coffee and dropped a fresh, cold glass of chocolate milk in front of Sadie.

"Is there anything else I can grab you?" she asked.

"Why don't you take the day off?" Colby said.

She shook her head. "Thanks, but I'm good."

"I mean, we're probably not going to be busy today," he said. "You could go to that guy's place and check it out. You'd be really good at designing a space."

She jerked her head back at the compliment. "Thanks, but I need to work this afternoon."

He furrowed his brow when she said that. She didn't mean to sound so needy, but Colby nodded and didn't ask another question. Which at that moment, she appreciated a lot, because she felt like everyone was telling her what to do.

"Are you sure?" he asked.

"My sister and father are having a double date tonight, and I'll be the fifth wheel." She nodded. "I'll work all night at the market."

Colby laughed at this, which did something to him. Made him even more handsome than the angry lumberjack look did.

"I wish I could go on a date," Sadie complained, rolling her eyes up to the ceiling.

Remy tilted her head at the young girl with heavily applied concealer and an orangish looking fake tan. "Ah, don't waste your time on boys. Find something that makes you happy first, then worry about a guy."

Sadie looked disappointed at Remy's answer. "Did you date boys at my age?"

"I didn't let her out of the house until she was eighteen," Gordon said from his seat. The couple that had been in between them had left.

"Well, Brady Mara wants to take me to the movies and my lame-o uncle won't let me go." This made Sadie roll her eyes even farther back into her head.

Then Remy contemplated the fact that she had less of a life than a thirteen-year-old. "Right, well, you have plenty of time to worry about guys."

"That's what everyone says, but Brady's going to high school next year, and I'll be stuck at the middle school for another whole year. If we can't see each other, he'll forget about me by the time I get there."

Remy would be lying if she said she didn't understand the girl's dramatics, because sadly she'd been Sadie at her age. She'd been the definition of boy crazy. She could still remember those strange teenage feelings. She had loved having crushes and liking boys. She had loved dating and having boyfriends—just loved love at that point in her life. She had watched every rom-com, read every romance book, listened to every love song ever written, on repeat. So, when she had met Joe, she hadn't wanted to see all the red flags that would ruin her fantasy.

"Excuse me, can we get seated?" a customer said from the front of the diner.

"It's seat yourself, but let me set you up in the booth if you'd like," Remy said, walking the older couple to the open booth against the windows. "The best seat in the diner."

More and more customers came in, and before Remy realized, Sadie was waving goodbye.

"Bye, Remy!" Sadie's hand fluttered back and forth.

"Bye, Sadie!" Remy waved back, smiling at the young girl, who might be her only friend in Blueberry Bay at this point, besides Emil.

"He's a doll, that one," Lindy said.

"Yes, Sadie's adorable," Remy said, thinking she hadn't heard Lindy right.

"Sadie, too." Lindy winked.

Remy shook her head. "I'm staying far away from all males. Unless, of course, it's a cat."

Lindy laughed. "I've been saying that my whole life. Wish I would have listened after four husbands."

"Four husbands!" Remy didn't mean to say it so loudly.

"They all were good men, just not good for me." Lindy shrugged. "I'm pretty picky."

"I guess so." Remy laughed at Lindy as she walked away.

She knew one thing for sure—if she were to ever get married again, it better be for the last time.

CHAPTER 14

After overhearing Remy's interaction with that Roland character, Colby had decided not to bother her by asking more about her ideas for the market. Besides, he didn't know how to ask without feeling like he was taking advantage of her goodwill. She obviously wanted to be paid for her ideas, and here he was trying to get them for free.

He came up with this long speech to offer to pay for her services, but then she showed up with a huge box in her hands.

"What's this?" he asked.

"I made a couple versions of baskets for the charcuteries," she said, opening the box. She pulled out red-and-white checkered fabric baskets with different types of glass jars and small pack-aged cracker boxes and waxed cheeses.

"Is that caviar?" Colby picked up a jar from the first basket.

"And uni roe, along with mignonette sauce for oysters, lemons, and locally grown fresh herbs." She pointed to a tiny glass jar. "I also made a crab cheese spread with the crab from yesterday's catch, a pickled cucumber salad, and added really great olives. I put in a dry local Chardonnay to compliment all the flavors. Oh, and a French baguette."

"I thought charcuteries were crackers and cheese." He picked up a glass bottle with a familiar reddish color inside. "You added cocktail sauce?" It was a different brand than they had carried.

"Good cocktail sauce," she said, plucking the bottle from his hands and placing it back into the basket. "Charcuterie is about fresh ingredients. You could call this basket a sea-cuterie."

He cringed inside at the cheesy name but kept his feelings to himself. "Do you really think someone's going to want to spend the money on all of this while buying lobsters?" He didn't think so.

"People come to Blueberry Bay to get away and celebrate life," Remy said. "They want to spend their money on good food that they don't normally get."

Was she right?

"And the baskets?" He rubbed his fingers along the fabric. "They must've cost a fortune."

She shook her head. "I sewed them together in like five minutes."

"You made these?" He picked one up. They were steadier than he expected.

She nodded.

The bell on the front door hit the glass, and a couple came into the market.

"Hello, can we help you?" Remy asked.

"We're here for the lobster!" the gentleman said with gusto.

"Well, you came to the right place."

"Oh, Don, look," the woman said, passing the baskets. "Do you think we should pick something like this up for when Gail and Jean come?"

The man tapped his chin with his finger, then nodded. "That's a good idea."

Remy pulled out a notecard from the basket. "Here's a list of the extras you'll want to grab at the fish counter."

"You carry fresh oysters?" The woman looked impressed.

Remy nodded. "Only fresh."

This made the woman happier, Colby noticed.

"How are you folks doing today?" Colby asked as they walked up to the counter. "You here visiting?"

The couple nodded. "We're staying at the Blueberry Bay Cottages," she said. "Oh, is that the Jacob O'Neill?" She pointed to the mural. "We heard about it at the front desk."

Colby nodded. "His only mural that we know of."

"It's gorgeous." She pulled out her phone. "Do you mind?"

He shot a look over to Remy, who was on her phone. He wasn't sure what the etiquette was in terms of photographing the mural, especially since the man who had painted it had a deeper connection with her than with him.

"Go ahead," he said, hoping Remy wouldn't get upset.

The husband gave the order of seven lobsters and two pounds of oysters. Colby was almost certain they'd buck at the price of everything, but the couple didn't even bat an eye when Remy told them their total.

"We're definitely coming back!" the woman said as they left with their purchases.

He looked at the rest of the baskets. The others were different, with other assorted items. "This must have taken forever."

She shrugged. "It passed the time."

"So I can offer three different types?" he asked, looking at the different baskets. She had cards, each with a title and a list of all the ingredients, along with suggested fish from the market. It was brilliant.

She shook her head. "The idea is to customize these to fit the freshest catch."

This made him grimace. He couldn't put these together without a guide. "Do you have suggestions?" He wanted to hit himself in the forehead. "I mean, do you think I could pay you to create these for me?"

"Sure," she said right away. "I can make more. Do you want them like I have?"

"I'd feel more comfortable with some that have lower price

points," he said, noticing the three figures that the last basket had cost them.

She nodded. "I can do that. I enjoy that kind of thing. Planning and organizing things."

She held out her hands at the store. He looked around, not realizing that throughout the day, she had rearranged what he'd put on the shelves. As irritating as it was that she'd done it without even asking, the way she put things together made complete sense.

"And if you were to make more changes," he started off, "what would you focus on next?"

She crossed her arms, looking around the space. "That would be more than just a few suggestions."

He really couldn't afford a designer like her, but something about her vision for the market felt right. Completely right. Now that she had pointed out their faults, it was like he couldn't unsee them. Like trying to get toothpaste back into the tube. He couldn't stop noticing all the things that needed to change. But he didn't know where to start or how to fix it like she did.

She looked away suddenly and tapped her fingers on the counter. "You're not just doing this because you overheard my conversation with my dad?"

He shook his head. "No, not at all." He stuffed his hands into his pockets. He wasn't one to go sharing his story, but the truth needed to be said. "I'm Sadie's guardian until my sister gets clean. And since she'll never get clean, that means I have to keep this place afloat until Sadie can take care of herself, which will probably be in her thirties with the way things are going."

She didn't move or look away, but he could tell she felt as uncomfortable as he did. Maybe because he made her feel that uncomfortable.

"Look, I'm sorry I was such a jerk when you first started," he said. "I'm not supposed to be working with people. I'm supposed to be out there fishing by myself."

He pointed out toward the ocean. The place where he felt

most himself. The Atlantic's mighty waters did something that nothing else in his life could—calm him. Life always carried a level of anxiety for Colby, an undercurrent that never left unless lulled by the waves.

"You're the one fishing for all this?" she asked.

He shook his head. "I used to be one of the fleets that brought in catch."

Her eyes looked up at him. "Really? What was that like?"

He let out a solitary sad laugh. "Perfect."

She leaned her elbows on the counter, resting her head in her hand. "Were you ever scared?"

He looked at the mural, knowing what she was getting at. He shook his head. "It's not like it used to be back in the day. The radar is so much better, the radios...communication in general is at a whole other level than when Jacob was out there." He paused, thinking of how to explain it. "It's like what he must've felt painting. I have to be present out there, and all the other stuff just floats away."

She looked out the windows at the water. "That sounds perfect."

They stared in silence for a long time, but he didn't feel the need to fill the quiet with chatter. He enjoyed the idea of her thinking fishing would be perfect, considering she turned her nose up at the idea of working in a market at first.

"My mom used to call that moment magical." Remy smiled. "She painted like Jacob and would get lost in her work for hours."

"That's what I imagine it would be like," he said. "I've never been creative." He lifted one of the corners of the basket. "I would never be able to put something like this together."

Remy stood up and crossed her arms. "I can help."

The bell rang again as a woman came into the market, and the phone began to ring.

"I would really appreciate it," Colby said.

She lifted the phone and answered it. "Harbor Market. How can I help you?"

Colby left the front and went back to the fish counter. He could hear his father talking to a fisherman who had just brought in his catch from the morning's take.

"We're going to be looking to triple the stock for more oysters," he said to the fisherman.

Emil rubbed his beard. "Oysters? When have we carried that many oysters?"

"Remy's suggesting that we do," he said, as though that should be enough of an explanation. "I think she's right. We need to start catering to the customers coming into the community, not the community that catches their own lobsters."

It made so much sense. Why hadn't they seen it before?

"Wholesale, restaurants, and mail orders," he added. "We need to think bigger now."

Emil nodded. "You know how I feel about the market."

Unfortunately, Colby's whole life had changed because of that feeling. Emil would never sell the market unless he had no other choice. And he'd never give up on his family.

"Have you heard from her?" Emil asked, not saying *her* name. His parents didn't say his ex-wife's name too often.

Colby shook his head. "It's done, Dad."

"There's always time," Emil said, ready to share his wisdom. "I've always found time is the best kind of healer."

Colby took in a deep breath, embracing for the inevitable story, but nothing would change the fact that Melanie was halfway across the world.

Suddenly, Remy came over to them. "I sold another basket."

Colby couldn't believe it. "Really?"

She laughed into her hands. "I know!"

"Do you think you could help me with ordering for the baskets?" he asked, handing her a catalog from one of their suppliers for the grocery items.

She didn't take it. "Yes. But for starters, I'll have to show you where you should order from."

CHAPTER 15

*G*inny walked into the market with Remy and greeted Emil and Colby with a hug. "I can't believe we haven't joined forces before."

Emil patted Ginny's back with both of his hands. "Lucy sends her regards."

"How's the new grandbaby?" Ginny asked.

"Number two," Emil said. "Can you believe we're this old?"

"When I wake up, yes I do," Ginny joked and gave a hearty pat on Emil's arm.

It wasn't a surprise to Remy that Gordon had fallen for Ginny. Her friendly demeanor, overly generous nature, and thoughtful disposition reminded her a lot of her mom. Jacqueline had that magnetizing personality people just gravitated toward.

Remy thought she had that charisma, that charm. The ability to put people at ease in her presence. In college, and even out in her first job at a museum, she seemed to have plenty of friends and people to surround her. She would often be invited out, offered to have drinks, included in plans. Now, she had no friends besides her sister, father and now Sadie. All the others in Blueberry Bay weren't really her friends.

If someone called the house, it was for Meredith or Gordon.

Greg occasionally texted but hadn't come back to Blueberry Bay since the auction and hadn't invited her back to Boston to stay at his place. Not that he had to, but none of her supposed friends from her old life had even called to see how she was doing. Did they even know about the divorce and move?

And there was the problem. She had been the one who had changed, like Joe said. She was a different person. But that was what losing a child did to someone. She wanted to cry! She wanted to scream! But Joe wanted silence. So, silence she gave him.

At the parties, he'd mingle around, talking business with everyone, and she'd stand in the peripheral, ignoring the women flirting with him. Not listening to the gossip being spoken about her. Ignoring the men checking her out. She'd just stand and wish for it to be over so she could go home and just lie in bed.

When Meredith had called that night about Jacob dying and inheriting his cottage, something had sparked inside her. She'd had to leave.

So, she had packed. She hadn't hidden what she was doing. When Joe had come to bed that night, after too many drinks and too many women boosting him up, he hadn't acted like he cared.

"You going somewhere?" he'd asked, his eyes blazing with alcohol.

She had been able to smell him from across the room.

"I'm going to stay with my sister for the summer," she'd said. "She needs my help with her father's estate."

"Her father left her something?" Joe's interest had been sparked. "What are we talking here?"

Remy had zipped up the suitcase, then sat on the bed. "I'm leaving, Joe."

"Tonight?" he'd asked.

"I need some space to think about things." She had waited to let the information sink in, her nerves itching up her back as she waited for his response.

But he hadn't said anything. He'd sat down on the bed, unbuttoned his shirt, and proceeded to get undressed, throwing his clothes into a heap on the floor before getting into bed. He'd either been too drunk to understand the severity of her statement or hadn't cared.

When he hadn't called the next day or the day after that, she had known he didn't care. He wasn't going to fight for her. And if he hadn't been willing to talk to her the night she had left him, why had she thought he'd be any different when he had shown up at the auction? He hadn't even bought a painting. He'd had no intention of changing, and Remy couldn't go back. She might have been sad and lonely and isolated in this little village, but she had independence. She might be broke and have to depend on Meredith and Gordon, but she didn't have to answer to Joe.

"Her full name is Camden Lucy," Emil told Ginny, while showing pictures on his phone.

"How's Bridgette?" Ginny asked.

"Good. Tired, but good," Emil said. "Lucy's been helping her out."

Ginny nodded and said, "You let us know when we can help out with babysitting."

"You let Bridgette know when you're willing, and I'm sure she'll be happy to have a free afternoon to take a nap," Emil said.

Remy hadn't thought about offering her time to help babysit. "I can too," she said. "I just love babies and would love to help."

Emil lifted his hands together in a clap. "I'll let her know."

"Ah, Ginny," Colby said, coming out from the back. "Thank you so much for coming by."

"I've got a bunch of different things to look at," Ginny said, carrying a crate with different homemade items that individual Queen Bees had made.

"I also took the liberty to call a few of the wineries I had visited over the summer to see if they were interested in selling their wine here," she said.

Colby put his hand through his hair, and it threw her off balance for some reason. The more time she spent around Colby, the more handsome he became to her. Something about the way he invested so much into his family without second-guessing his decision to leave fishing made him much sexier to her, especially after seeing him at the diner eating with Sadie. The fact that he'd gone out and bought the bracelet for his niece for her period made him...

She shook the thought away before it developed— that he was the kind of man she wanted in her life.

"What kind of products do you think would work?" he asked, looking into the crate. There were blueberry jams and jellies, honey, and maple syrup. "Are these candles?"

"Yes, made from beeswax," Ginny said, putting her hands on her hips. "And here's a list of baked goods we can make if you want to order ahead of time."

Ginny handed Colby a list written on a piece of paper with bees floating around in the top margin. The Queen Bees even had a letterhead?

"What do you think?" Colby asked Remy.

Remy peeked at the list of goods. She felt strange being considered an expert on what to sell at a market, but she had attended enough gatherings to know what was being passed around on trays and at dinner. She knew that people on vacation wanted wine and fancy drinks. They wanted finger food that paired well with a lobster dinner. They wanted a homecooked country meal with Boston ingredients. They wanted organic, fresh, and trendy.

"I'd go with the jams and jellies, the honey, some of the baked goods like breads and desserts, but not the muffins or things like that." Remy went through the list, using a pencil to check off the items she thought would sell.

Ginny gave her opinion on items along with tidbits of information about the creator.

"She's just had hip surgery," Ginny said when they asked about the beeswax candle. "But she should have enough in stock for now."

"People are really going to buy a candle?" Colby looked doubtful.

"If it's labeled with Harbor Market, Blueberry Bay, then yes," Remy said. "This will remind them of their vacation when they stayed at the beach and had a lobster bake. It will be like any other destination during their stay."

Colby cocked his head and stared at her. His penetrating stare made her cheeks heat up, and she couldn't tear her eyes away.

"I love that idea," he said.

And her heart skipped a beat.

She immediately looked down at her hands, still holding the pencil, and circled where the candles were listed a few times. "Great."

She looked at her phone, sweat accumulating on the small of her back and her chest. "I should be going."

Ginny looked up from the list, along with Emil. "You're leaving already?"

She nodded, backing away from the three of them standing together. "I have to meet someone. Let me know if you need anything else before my shift on Tuesday."

Colby nodded. The look that made her knees wobble had vanished. Now the crease in his forehead had returned, and the hard lines deepened on his face. Knowing a little more about Colby's situation, she understood the rough exterior and short temper. The man carried his whole family on his shoulders.

And for some reason, that made him very attractive.

She needed to get out of there before she made a fool of herself.

She backed out of the store, waving to the group, and walked to the address that Roland had texted. It was only a mile from the harbor, and she didn't mind the walk to clear her head.

She followed Main Street along the harbor's edge and took a right down Ocean Avenue. The road had no sidewalk, but no cars either. Once out of the main strip of the village, Blueberry Bay was a quiet place.

To the right of Remy was Blueberry Bay and the great Atlantic Ocean spanning out as far as the eye could see. In between houses, she would peek through the yards out at the water. On this side of the bay, most of the waterfront had been built on. She saw no blueberry bushes on this end of town. She looked across the bay to see if the cottage was in view, but she couldn't see it.

As she walked, she listened to the waves and the cries of seagulls. Focusing her thoughts on the next moment, not the what-ifs. She had too many negative what-ifs. What if he thought she was an idiot and that her ideas were stupid? What if she came across as needy and pathetic? What if he really just wanted a date, and when he got the hint, he'd just fire her?

She stopped at a public vista spot. A plaque stood on the edge of the granite cliffs, dedicated to those lost at sea. The view was one she hadn't seen before. It overlooked the harbor and the blueberry fields of Jacob's farm. From that spot, she felt so small and insignificant, and so did her problems.

She kept her focus on the lighthouse off in the distance. The white-and-red tower sat alone on a rock island covered in birds and pines. She had an urge to paint, to capture that moment right then, to keep that feeling she had in her chest, that feeling of pride. She was changing. She was going to make her dreams happen. She would not let life pass her by but take what time she had left and do what she wanted. Not wait for others to tell her it was okay.

She inhaled a long breath, closing her eyes. She would make things happen. She exhaled slowly, listening to the wave's rhythm against the rocks below.

She would make things happen.

She took off for Roland's place. The modern architecture stood out among the traditional clapboard cottages that surrounded it. The sleek, straight lines and contemporary angles would clearly showcase the ocean, she determined, even before stepping inside. The whole back end was a wall of glass.

She texted Roland as she came up his driveway, and he opened the door almost immediately. "You walked?"

He looked around the yard for a car.

She held up her hands. "I wanted to take in the beautiful day."

With the sun out, this seemed to please him. She didn't need to tell him that she couldn't afford the oil for her oil change.

"Come in," he said, opening the glass double doors to the house.

Remy had been in many beautifully designed homes throughout her life. Her parents had lived in a classical colonial home, she had lived in homes built by some of the most prestigious builders in New England, and Roland's house still took her breath away.

"This place is incredible!" she said, walking into the space. "How high are these ceilings?"

"Twenty feet," he said.

She thought of the heating costs. "I thought my sister's view was amazing."

This made Roland stand with pride. She could tell he enjoyed showing off his place. "I had a Norwegian architect come out to Maine and look at the land before he drew up his plans."

"Wow," she said, impressed and unimpressed all the same. Had he done it for the design or so he could brag about it? She'd met many people who enjoyed telling the story of what lengths they went through for the perfect counter or chandelier or fixture instead of just loving the counter or chandelier or fixture for its beauty. Like someone buying a house on the ocean without truly loving the water and cliffs and sounds that came with it.

Inside, the house showcased the ocean with a wall of windows, but the lack of anything personal made the space feel commercial rather than like a living space. From the floors to the hardware, nothing felt personal. The view, which should have been the focal point, felt more like a background.

He opened the glass doors, which folded into each other, opening up the inside to the outside.

"Oh, wow," she said, stepping out onto the deck. "I feel like I'm looking out at the whole world."

"Pretty much," he said. "That's why I had to buy the land when I saw it for sale. I wanted to stand on the edge of the world like Jack in *Titanic*."

From the outside, the house didn't add anything to the coastline but kind of stuck out from the other more traditional fishermen's cottages. It didn't fit into the landscaping like most Norwegian design was meant to; it almost went against it, sticking its decking out over the granite ledges and drawing the eyes up to the high roofline rather than the tips of the pine trees that Maine's coastline was known for.

As gorgeous as the house was, it felt unwelcoming and empty. Only a black leather couch and set of chairs sat in the middle of the living room. The dining room had a long rectangular table with a bowl of fake fruit.

"Are you a minimalist?" she asked, looking for Jacob's painting that he'd bought.

Roland held his hand behind her back, gesturing her down the deck toward where he opened another set of glass doors and led her into the kitchen. His hand was close enough that she could feel it against the fabric of her shirt, but he didn't touch her.

The gesture felt polite and respectful, but more friendly than just business acquaintances.

She stepped through the doors quickly, hoping he'd take the hint. She just wanted to be business acquaintances. When he came into the room, he stepped away from her and around the large marble waterfall kitchen island that ran the length of the whole room.

"Now that's a kitchen island," she said.

"I put this in for my mother," he said. "She loves to cook."

"Is this a second home for her, too?" she asked, trying to think of ideas for the kitchen design. She had talked to Greg, who had told her Roland was a very eligible bachelor who was a commercial real estate broker. She had been thinking this would be more of a bachelor pad design over a beach cottage, but if he had family coming... "What were you thinking?"

"Clean. Smooth. Like a good whiskey," he said. "My mother will come up for visits, but this will be my retreat."

"Right," she said, regretting taking the job. She hated whiskey.

"What are you thinking right away?" he asked, excited to hear her ideas for his perfect space.

She stepped through the kitchen. "You have the most beautiful view, yet nowhere to really enjoy it."

She turned around, raising her arms towards the mostly empty room. "Minimalism works in a condo in Cambridge, not on the edge of the water. You want to have seating and lots of it. It's warm out, but I'm cold in here."

"Yikes, that's really harsh," he said.

She covered her mouth with her hand. "Sorry."

He lifted his eyebrows, leaning against the counter. "I want this place to be welcoming."

"It's not." She'd said it too quickly.

"You're very honest," he said, crossing his arms against his chest.

She ran her hand along the cold marble. "It's a beautiful house, it just hasn't been dressed up yet."

"What would you do first?" he asked.

Remy realized that was the second time that day someone had asked her opinion. And each time, she didn't hesitate, because she knew exactly what she would do first.

"I'd put cedar shingling along the ceiling, drawing the eye away from the height and out to the ocean." The tall ceiling was white, which did nothing but draw the eye away from the water. "Then I'd take that gas fireplace out and hire a quality mason to build you a massive stone woodfire burning one instead."

"You don't like my fireplace?" He dropped his hands by his

side and walked into the living room. "Do you like anything about the house?"

"The view." She turned her back to the wall of windows, examining the room. "Look, I just think you forgot you were in Down East, Maine."

"I don't want to live in an L.L.Bean catalogue and have a stuffed moose above the fireplace," he said.

"How about a bear?" she said and laughed at her own joke. "I'm just talking about a few cosmetic changes to draw the beauty of the natural elements from outside into your space. It's very Norwegian."

He gave her a sly side-eye glance.

"How long have you been in real estate?" she asked, thinking about when she had first gotten her "career" job in the museum.

"Over fifteen years," he said. "I started off in accounting, but everyone just sat in their cubicle crunching numbers." He shook his head as he sipped his wine. "I hated it. Then I had this uncle who had commercial properties that he asked me to take care of, and before I knew it, I was buying my first property and then my next. I soon had over a dozen properties and rentals. I bought a storage unit business, then I got my real estate license, and here we are."

"You did really well for yourself." She was impressed for sure. "This is truly a beautiful house."

"Thank you," he said, holding his glass of wine to her.

She took a sip of her own. "Where's Jacob's painting?"

She hadn't seen it anywhere in the house.

"I have it in my office back in Boston," he said. "I love looking at it, dreaming of being here."

She smiled, knowing exactly how he felt. "I don't miss the city at all."

"Not even a little?" he asked.

She thought about it for a long time, racing through the memories of living with Joe in the heart of the city near Beacon Hill. "No. Not one bit."

"I went to prep school down the road in a town close by." He said this as if that made him a local. "I just love the coastline of Maine. So gorgeous. Do you think you could make this house as gorgeous as the coastline?"

She looked around. It had huge potential if she leaned into the bones of the structure, but she wasn't a professional. She had no idea what it would cost, if she could even find people to help her. Would she be able to find the right materials along with the right pieces? She was fooling herself if she thought she could make this house what he wanted. The guy clearly had a different perspective of style than her, but what were her options?

This could be her big break. And she needed one of those right about now.

"Absolutely."

CHAPTER 16

*R*emy hadn't expected to have such a nice time with Roland, but she had. They'd talked for hours about different designs and ideas. He had opened another bottle of wine and they'd sat like old friends telling stories about college and first job experiences. He had even walked her all the way back to town and waited until Meredith had picked her up.

She had to admit she liked him, and more than just for business. By the end of the night, she might have kissed him if he had gone for it, but thankfully nothing had happened and she didn't have anything to regret. Not that she was someone who'd do something she'd regret, but a kiss would complicate a lot of things. She had a plan and she needed to stick to it.

"So...?" Meredith asked at dinner the next night.

"So....?" Remy said back, pretending not to know what she was referring to. "You've been smiling all day, you talked on the phone for an hour, and he swung by work, I heard."

"How'd you hear that?"

"Ginny," Meredith said. She lifted her eyebrows up and down. "So...?"

"So, nothing." She got up from the table, carrying her plate to the sink. She had brought home some of the biggest and most delicious scallops she had ever tasted in her life. "Those scallops were so good. Emil told me to just use olive oil, a touch of lemon, and a dash of salt. Nothing else."

"But do you like him enough to maybe see him, other than to talk about the house?" Meredith asked.

Remy shook her head. "I have plans and they do not include getting involved with someone."

"You never know. I mean, look at Quinn and me or Dad and Ginny," Meredith said.

How could she not? They were everywhere lately. "I know and I'm really happy for all of you, but right now I've set some goals for myself, and I want to just focus on them."

That night, she went to bed and opened her bank account app on her phone. She hadn't been working for very long, but already she was earning a little nest egg. She understood she was fortunate to be able to stay with family and that it was the real reason she could save so much, but as of right now, she had enough for first and last month's rent.

And if she continued to earn what she had been, she could afford at least a small two bedroom.

The next morning, she opened the diner with Lindy.

"You're looking for a rental?" Lindy said when she saw Remy looking at the ads.

Remy nodded. "Know of anyone renting out a place?"

"You know, *you* do," Lindy said, pointing at her.

"Me?" Remy hoped she didn't mean Meredith.

"Colby St. Germain's been trying to rent out his house since his wife left him," Lindy said.

"What?" Remy's mouth dropped.

"Oh." Lindy put her hand on her hip. "You haven't heard about the ex."

Remy shook her head. "No. I didn't know he had even been married."

"Happy, too, as far as I knew," Lindy said. "You'd see them

together at church and public events, but then one day, poof! She vanished. Went to London and never looked back."

"Wow." Remy thought her situation was bad. "Just like that?"

"Just like that." Lindy tsked her tongue. "Shame, too. They were good together. A little hometown couple."

How many love songs were written about that kind of scenario? "Poor guy."

"He's been trying to find someone to rent the place year-round instead of just tourists in and out all summer," Lindy said. "You should talk to him."

"Yeah, maybe." It would be so easy to just run over during her break and ask about it, but something about asking Colby for something more…she just couldn't. And having "Don't park in the loading zone," as her landlord? No, thanks.

"It's over by your side of the bay, right on Beach Plum Lane," Lindy said, grabbing a plate for table six. "Cute little white house."

Remy put her hand on Lindy's arm to catch her attention before she left. "Is it the one up on the hill? With the porch?"

"That's the one." Lindy swung the plate up into the air and took off.

Throughout the day, she thought about the house. She adored the tiny fisherman's house. Right on the edge of town, it sat on the corner of Main Street and Beach Plum Lane. Two miles from Meredith, a walk from downtown, and across the street from the water.

She ran to the market.

Colby stopped sweeping as soon as she came into the store. She stopped and stepped back onto the front porch, noticing the planters and newly placed window boxes.

"Did you build those yourself?" she asked.

Colby nodded. "I've been working on them at home. I still have to paint them."

She couldn't believe how nice of a job he had done. "They look great."

"I got pansies for now," he said. He had listened to everything she'd suggested so far, even down to the seasonal flowers.

"Easter is just around the corner," she said.

"And my shipment of coffee and teas came in," he said, walking toward the shelves where a new coffee grinder sat.

"People love good coffee, and they can't find it anywhere around here," she whispered. "Don't tell Lindy."

"You're right," he said. "I hate the city, but I do love being able to get good coffee."

"Freshly ground coffee," she said back.

"I sold all the baskets," Colby said. Then he looked at his watch. "Are you working today?"

She shook her head, feeling slightly nervous about asking about the house. She didn't know what about this man made her nervous. He seemed a bit full of himself, even if he had an altruistic heart of gold. "I heard you have a rental property?"

"Are you looking for a new place?" he asked.

She clasped her hands together, hoping the price was reasonable. "Only if I can afford it."

She gave him a small smile. This could be the beginning of her new life. Her new journey.

"What can you afford?" he asked, being vague, which made her nervous.

"Half my paycheck?' Though she knew from growing up with Gordon that was too much.

"How about this?" Colby took a pen and scribbled down some numbers. "This is the monthly rent. Heat and utilities are included."

"Seriously?" The number looked way too low. "This is how much you charge for a whole house?"

"This is northern Maine, not Boston." He dug his hand into his pocket. "Let me show you it."

"Really?" She put her hand to her mouth. "Yes! Are you serious?"

"Yeah, come on," he said.

"But you could probably get ten times that during the summer," she said.

"And have to keep up with all the damages the influx of families cause for weekly beach rentals," he said. "My family has a few beach rentals already, and it's a lot of upkeep and work and it sits empty most of the time. Plus, people cancel and weather is finicky and having a stable renter would be less stressful."

"Wow, I guess so," she said, thinking about it all.

"Come on," he said. "I'll drive."

She followed him out to the parking lot and got into the truck. She could smell his aftershave as soon as she got inside the cab. Hair ties and pink sunglasses sat on the seat, and she put them into the cup holder.

"Sadie's things," he said to her.

She smiled and looked out the window as he drove down Main Street to the corner of Beach Plum Lane.

She gasped as he pulled into the drive. "It's so cute."

The traditional fisherman's farmhouse had two stories, with a pitched roof tall enough for a window and what she assumed was an attic and probably the best view in the house. The front had steps leading to a porch that ran the width of the house. In the back, the house extended and had its own side entrance and porch. This place had a ton of character but was also a blank canvas.

"Let's go inside," Colby said, shutting off his truck.

She jumped out and followed him to the back, peeking into the windows as she walked by. There didn't appear to be much landscaping, but she was already imagining flower and vegetable gardens.

"The house is old, but I've updated most of the appliances," he said, stepping onto the porch and opening the screen door.

Remy turned to look out at the view. She could see the water from where she stood, and she saw the best view was from the front porch. She imagined a swinging chair where she could sit and watch the sunrise each morning.

Colby jingled the key in the lock and popped the door open. Inside, warm honey pine floors greeted them as they stepped over the threshold.

She immediately began taking off her shoes.

"Don't worry about it, really," he said. "The place needs to be cleaned up anyway. It's been empty all winter."

She stepped into what appeared to be the mudroom. She noticed a door that led to a small half bath. She turned and walked down the hall into the kitchen.

"Oh, wow," she said. Not only had Colby replaced the appliances, but he chose state-of-the-art replacements. "You didn't hold back."

"I was fishing when I renovated this place," he said.

She didn't know what kind of money fishermen brought in with lobster, but they obviously did well.

She ran her hand against the quartz countertops. "I love the design."

She couldn't believe how beautiful the place was. On one end, there were exposed shelves, and the other held a built-in glass China cabinet. To her amazement, a cast iron range sat against the interior wall.

"Tell me it still works," she said, already obsessed with the place.

"It still works." He stepped around the butcher block in the middle of the kitchen. "You want to keep looking?"

"Uh, yes," she said, blowing past him to the dining room. A table and eight chairs sat in the middle. "Does the furniture stay?"

She'd need a few things herself.

He nodded. "For now."

"Right." She walked through to the living room. Another woodstove fireplace, she noted. "Do they all work?"

"That's how you'll get a lot of your heat in the winter," he said. "If you take it."

She didn't even have to look further once she saw the picture window looking out front to the harbor and Blueberry Bay below.

"I'll take it," she said.

"You haven't even seen the rest of the house."

"I love it," she said.

He nodded, then took his keys out of his pocket and removed one from the ring. He handed it over to her. "Looks like you have a new place to decorate."

CHAPTER 17

"Why are you rushing to get out of the cottage?" Meredith clearly didn't understand. "You can stay as long as you like."

Gordon looked as surprised as Meredith.

"I want to start a family," Remy said honestly. "I've been waiting to start one for a long time now, and well, it's time."

This seemed to shock Meredith and Gordon into silence.

"Are you getting a sperm donor?" Gordon asked, trying to put all the information together.

Remy shook her head. "I want to be a foster mother."

Gordon's forehead wrinkled. "That's really honorable of you, Remy, but taking in a foster kid...that's a lot."

"Yes, I know," she said. "But I've been working, and I've saved all my alimony." Remy wasn't completely broke anymore. She had some cash. "I know I could save money by staying with you, but I'm forty-five. I'm not getting any younger. If I have to work two jobs, then I have to work two jobs. But for now, this is what I want to do."

"It's a huge commitment," Meredith said. "If you stay here, we can help you."

"You've already raised your kids, and so has Dad," Remy said.

She wouldn't stay at the cottage with or without fostering a child. The glaring fact is that for Meredith's life to move forward, Remy needed to leave. It was that simple. She'd made up her mind. "I know this seems completely out of left field, but I've been thinking about this for years and I'm ready. I can't wait any longer. I need to do this."

"I just think you're rushing a bit." Meredith looked at Gordon.

"I think we should go check out your new place," Gordon said, giving Remy a wink. "I think it's great what you want to do. Our family could use a little growing."

Remy didn't know why she became emotional, but she wrapped her arms around her father. "I wish Mom was here."

"Me too," Gordon said.

Remy held up the key. "Let me show you the house."

It took less than a ten-minute drive to the cottage and would be an easy enough walk.

"It's perfect," Meredith said. Her mouth gaped open at the front porch.

"It's mine...for now." Remy could feel her chest expanding. This would be her home. She was now a resident of Blueberry Bay.

"You know," Gordon said. "Grandpas make good roommates."

"I appreciate you saying that, but I want this and I want to do this on my own." That, Remy had been sure of since the day she had decided to leave Joe. She wanted a family and she'd do it herself if she needed to. "I'm good, really. I'm good."

Gordon nodded, then held out his hand. "After you."

Remy had butterflies in her stomach as she took out the key. "Let me show you inside."

She walked up the steps to the porch.

"Oh, Remy!" Meredith exclaimed. "The view!"

Remy took in the sight before unlocking the door. "Wait until you see the top floor's view."

From that point, Meredith and Gordon were on board with Remy's decision.

146

"You should come down to Massachusetts with me and choose some of the furniture you want to keep," Gordon said. "I think I'm going to put it on the market next month. Then have an outreach program come and collect the rest."

"Maybe some of Mom's art?" Meredith asked.

Gordon looked around the room. "Looks like Remy has a perfect spot for a few paintings."

Remy looked at her father and smiled. "I'd love that."

"And there's always room for a Jacob O'Neill or two," Meredith said, looking around the living room.

"I couldn't," Remy said, but she could feel that stretching in her chest, the excitement building up. "But I'd love that."

"I think the one of the lupine with the sunlight hitting it," Meredith said.

"A Ray of Hope." The title they had given it.

"Yes, that's the one," Meredith walked into the living room and turned in a circle. "This is a great space."

Remy couldn't agree more, feeling confident in her decision. "Let me show you upstairs and the attic."

"Let's go see the attic," Meredith said excitedly.

Remy decided to hold off on moving in until she had everything ready to go. She wanted to clean the house from top to bottom. She also wanted to change the electricity and gas over to her name. She needed to order a cord of wood for the rest of the spring for the woodstove, and she would need to get those chimneys swept before she started any fires. She wanted to clean out everything that she didn't need and store it in the basement. Then she wanted to decorate and paint. Well, if Colby would let her paint.

She wondered if she should text him when her phone began ringing in the kitchen. She ran through the empty house and grabbed it. "Hello?"

"Remy!" Roland said loudly on the phone. "I'm headed up from the city. Tell me you're free tonight to go over your ideas."

She had none. In fact, she had been so busy with working, and now with the rental, she hadn't even thought about Roland's space.

"I have a ton of ideas," she said, "but I don't have any final sketches."

"That's fine," Roland said. "Why don't I pick you up and we can talk over dinner?"

She sat silent for a moment, thinking what the best answer would be. In some weird way, Roland did interest her, and he was attractive on top of that. And she wanted this job. It could land her some interest from others. Word of mouth was huge in interior design. Location not so much now that things could be done virtually. Roland had deep pockets as well. She could really experiment with her design and create great spaces to showcase her ideas.

But she didn't want to give Roland the wrong impression either. She had made up her mind on foster care.

"Dinner to talk design, right?" she asked.

"Or maybe more than just design?" Roland said back.

"I'm starting a family," she blurted out, wishing she had thought about how to explain it to him better.

"You're pregnant?" he asked.

She shook her head even though he couldn't see. "No, I'm just starting to think about fostering a child. I was planning on starting the process once I move into my new home."

The line went silent for a moment. "That's so admirable."

"Thank you," she said, waiting for the "but."

"What made you decide on that path?" he said with a laugh. "No joke, I've been thinking about it myself. I don't have a family or anyone to pass on my legacy to. I also want to make a difference before I leave this place behind."

"You're kidding." Remy couldn't believe it. What were the chances she'd meet a single guy who loved art and wanted to foster a child? "That's incredible."

Roland and Remy talked for over an hour about their plans. He told her about wanting to give back. She told him about her miscarriages. She hadn't opened up like that in a long time and it felt good.

"So?" he asked. "Will you have dinner when I arrive?"

She had completely forgotten he was driving up to Blueberry Bay as they spoke. "Yes, I'd like that."

After a shower and hair and makeup, Remy stood in front of her closet looking for something to wear for her first date since Joe. She hadn't had another man touch her or kiss her or make love to her in over fifteen years. Fifteen years of marriage hadn't made them stronger in that department either. Joe was usually so stressed out that he didn't want to have alone time with her. Nothing personal, and Remy had required personal. So, he'd avoided her, especially when she'd lost the first baby. He had never come around the house unless there was an event or he'd been with associates and assistants. Not even when he'd come for the festival to work things out could he sit alone with her.

It was how the whole argument had started. If he couldn't sit with his wife and talk about their marriage, had they even had a marriage?

She pulled out the best dress she'd brought to Maine from the dozen couture gowns and pulled out a Chanel she had picked up in London. She loved that dress. She had worn it to dinner with Joe when they first got married. He had told her she looked beautiful in it.

Remy wanted to live her life for herself. And going on a date, talking about design, and dreaming about a future family sounded absolutely perfect at this stage in her life.

She should be excited about tonight.

But a nervous energy swept through her. What was she doing? Did this man expect something more than just a little dinner and design talk?

Oh goodness, she thought to herself when she heard the doorbell. She listened as Meredith quickly answered the door and welcomed Roland into the cottage.

"Can I get you something to drink?" Meredith asked. Remy

could hear the fridge pop open. "I have iced tea, water, and white wine. Remy will only be a few more minutes, I'm sure."

"I'm good, thanks," Roland replied. "This place is amazing. I'm across the bay and have always wondered about the little gray cottage on the ocean's cliffs."

"Let me show you around," Meredith said, and Remy could hear them walk into the dining room.

She put her hair into a small twist by the base of her neck. She looked at her reflection in the mirror. She looked refined yet stylish, exactly what Joe would've expected for a night like tonight had she been going to dinner with him.

Then Colby crossed her mind. What would she wear if she went out to dinner with Colby? She wouldn't wear that dress. Not because he wasn't fancy enough, but because she imagined that would be the last thing that would impress him.

What impressed Colby? Hard work, helpfulness, thoughtfulness, advice, and good organization. All things she also valued.

"Remy?" Meredith said from behind the bathroom door. "Are you going to be ready soon?"

Remy opened the door and met Roland downstairs.

"You look incredible," he said, taking her hand and kissing it.

"Thank you. So do you," she said, admiring his blue button-up that opened at the neck just enough to show off his chest. His khakis were fitted in just the right areas. On paper, Roland appeared perfect. So why wasn't she excited about going out to dinner with him? "Shall we?"

Colby struck her mind as she used the word *shall*.

"After you," Roland said, holding out his hand toward the door.

Gordon joked about not staying out late, but Remy couldn't remember the last time she had stayed out at all.

Remy didn't know why she was nervous, because Roland was a complete gentleman and they had wonderful conversations. She talked to him about her ideas and showed some of her sketches of what the space would look like, but she also asked him what he wanted. They talked about her growing up in Andover and how she had wanted to be an interior designer since she was a little girl.

"I'd rearrange my parents' furniture all the time." Remy had done it dozens of times by the time she'd left for college. "I love creating a space that creates a feeling of belonging. Where you want people to feel welcome to stay and be together."

"Hmm," Roland said. "Everything you've described about the design sounds perfect. You are quite fascinating, Remy O'Neill."

"Johnson," she corrected him. "My father's Gordon Johnson. The man you met."

Roland looked surprised. "You're not related to Jacob O'Neill? He's not your father?"

"No, he's Meredith's father," she explained. She thought he had known.

"Oh…" He looked down at his silverware. "I wish you had told me that."

"Why does it matter?" she asked.

Roland leaned back in his seat. "It doesn't, I guess."

But she could feel something shift between them. She thought back through their conversations. She swore she had explained their relationship. Hadn't he been told by Greg? "You met my father tonight. Gordon. The man who joked as we left."

"The man named Gordon is your father?" he asked. "I thought that was your sister's boyfriend."

Remy laughed at the thought. "He's seventy-five."

This only made Roland shrug.

"What about your family?" she asked.

"My father is in banking. My mother was also in real estate." Roland went through his family history of real estate adventures, starting with his grandfather, who had started with one piece of property in Lawrence, Massachusetts, and now they had twenty-six real estate offices across the New England area. "I work hard to keep my family's name a trusted name in real estate."

By the end of dessert, Remy had enjoyed their time together. "I love that you ordered every dessert on the menu."

She took her fork one last time and dug into a piece of cheesecake.

Roland spooned out the last of his crème brûlée. "I love dessert more than the dinner course."

"Hmm, me too." She almost said something about a next time, but stopped herself. She didn't want to rush things.

"What was being married to Joe Moretti like?" Roland asked.

The mention of Joe's name threw her completely off. One, she was certain she hadn't told him who her ex-husband was, which meant he had either known, looked her up, or found out from Greg. Maybe Greg had told him. She knew people Googled others, but she found it strange and intrusive. And if he already knew, why hadn't he said something?

"Do you know Joe?" she asked. Joe knew everyone.

"I know of him, through a friend of a friend," he said, wiping his face with the linen napkin before setting it onto the table. "Let me take care of the bill."

She smiled and thanked him, but something felt weird, and she couldn't put her finger on it.

"Would you like to come back to my place and we can open a bottle of wine?" he asked.

Remy could already feel the glass of wine she had at dinner and thought against it. "I'd love to, but I have an early shift tomorrow morning."

"Greg told me he really stuck it to you in the divorce." Roland shook his head. "You should've gotten a good attorney."

"No attorney can break an iron-clad prenup," she said dryly. Now she knew he had been talking to someone about her.

"Ah, that will do it," he said. "But necessary at times."

"I wouldn't know. I never wanted his money."

"I'm sure you didn't, but believe me when I say many people will do anything they can to live a certain lifestyle." Roland threw down his black platinum card. "I've dated a lot of women who expected more from our relationship because of my money."

"Yes, well, I'm not interested, to be honest."

He rested his elbow on the table and leaned over, close to her. "That's why you're so fascinating. You wait tables and you can spot a Jackson Pollock a hundred feet away."

"I may be able to spot one," she said, but she wasn't sure why that made her fascinating.

"Come back to my place." He leaned even closer.

"I really have to get up early," she said.

"Alright," he said, but he took her hand and kissed the top of it. "Tell me you'll have dinner with me again."

"Sure," she said then added, "and set up a time to look at some design structures, maybe go over some furniture choices?"

She could easily put some images together. She had enough of an idea of where she'd like to go.

"Yes, but dinner first," he said.

"That sounds good," she said, but she had a feeling he wasn't going to be asking about her designs any time soon.

When Roland dropped her off, he walked her up the front porch. He took her hand, and leaning slowly toward her, he kissed her softly on the cheek before saying goodnight.

"Goodnight, Remy," he said, stepping back.

"Goodnight, Roland," she said.

She stayed outside on the porch, watching him drive away before going inside.

"So?" Meredith asked, sitting in the living room with Quinn and watching a documentary.

"It was nice," Remy said, not adding any details.

"Uh-oh," Quinn said from the couch.

"What?" Remy asked.

"Nice means boring," he said, looking for confirmation from Meredith, who nodded, looking concerned in return.

"It *was* really nice, and then he asked me about Joe," she said, wishing she could talk to Meredith alone.

"Wait, what? He asked you about Joe?" Meredith asked, still half-focused on the documentary.

Remy didn't mind Quinn being there or talking to her. In fact, she liked Quinn a lot. She loved the fact that Meredith had fallen in love with him. They were good together. But at that moment, she'd kill to just have her sister alone to give her advice.

"I think I'll make myself a cup of tea," she said, not willing to share any more in front of Quinn.

"I heard congratulations are in order," Quinn said.

"Oh, yeah, I got myself a new place," she said.

"Oh, that too," Quinn said. "Meredith told me you might be fostering a child. That's really incredible."

"Thank you, Quinn," she said, shooting her eyes at Meredith, who was still focused on the screen. Remy was surprised Meredith had told him about it. Not that she had asked her sister to keep it a secret, but she hadn't expected she'd needed to. It was personal. But Meredith had entered the point of her relationship where anything personal was shared with Quinn. A wonderful spot to be in when in a relationship.

"I'm headed to bed." She walked up the stairs, not even waiting for her sister's response. She didn't even ask, but she could tell Gordon was with Ginny.

She decided to relax before bed. Before, she'd have taken a long bath to relax. Grabbed a glass of wine, a good book or magazine, and sat in there for as long as the water stayed warm. It was the one thing she did miss from her old lifestyle—her old master bathroom. Joe always made a point in whatever house they lived in to give her a beautiful bathroom. She would spend hours taking baths. She just loved a good soak. Jacob's bathrooms were cramped, drafty, and the tub didn't fit her. Meredith planned on renovating, but in order to create a beautiful bathroom, Remy needed to get out of the guest room.

She opened her journal and started with a new list of things she needed to get done. Her pen started drawing out floor plans for her things, want lists, and numbers to contact, including

Health and Human Services to set up an appointment to talk about fostering.

Was she ready for this next step?

She thought about Colby and how he had dropped his whole life to raise Sadie. She'd use him as inspiration. If Colby could do it and continue to help the way he did, so could she.

That was when Debra Fox appeared on the television, and the idea came to mind. Remy was certain that when the Boston arts and entertainment reporter had told Remy to contact her any time, she wasn't hoping for a story about a market but, the St. Germains deserved a bit of help as well.

She took out her phone and texted Debra with a picture of the mural.

An original mural by Jacob O'Neill.

It took Debra a second to respond. **Can I get a statement about your divorce?**

Remy's thumb hung above the letters. She didn't want to make a statement.

No statement.

The dots at the bottom flashed and then disappeared. So, that was that. Remy no longer held enough power to get the attention of the news. Her life being Joe Moretti's wife was officially over.

Then a text flashed on the screen. **I'll bring my crew up in the morning.**

Remy covered her mouth and laughed. She texted right back. **Great! See you then!**

Maybe she was more than just Mrs. Joe Moretti.

Maybe being Remy Johnson was enough.

CHAPTER 18

"Can I please skip school?" Sadie pleaded with prayer hands in the driver's seat. "How could you let your niece miss her opportunity to be on national television?"

"First of all, it's a Boston channel, so none of your friends are going to see it," Colby said, still in complete disbelief that a news station wanted to drive all the way up from Boston for a mural, but he'd take the free publicity any day. "Second, you have school."

"Come on, brah," she said, a new expression that had developed in the middle school.

"They only want to talk to Gramps anyway," Colby said.

"Sheesh," answered Sadie. Another annoying expression developed among thirteen-year-olds.

"They're talking to Gramps and maybe Remy," he added.

"You should do something nice for her," Sadie said.

He completely agreed. "You have an idea?"

"Something to say thank you but also to say *I like you*," Sadie said as he turned on Hemlock toward the school. "Then throughout the day, you just nonchalantly start asking personal questions about her and what she likes to do. My app says she'll start falling in love with you within two weeks."

Colby stretched out in his seat and rested on the console, listening to his niece, who was wise beyond her thirteen years, but he also didn't pay real attention to her hundredth lecture on how to land Remy before she fell for the rich guy down the road.

"I hate to break it to you, Sadie, but she wants nothing to do with me," Colby said.

"That's not true," Sadie said. "I saw the look."

"The look?" he asked, wondering if his niece was really onto something or if she was just as crazy as the rest of the women in his family.

"Yes, the look," she huffed. "She was giving you that look. Like she has a crush on you."

He laughed at the idea. "I think she hates me."

"Isn't that what you said when Joey Miller hit me in the head with a soccer ball?" Sadie turned up the volume on the radio to the point the bass could be heard from outside.

"Come on, Sadie, do we have to listen to this song again?" he said, changing the subject.

"Yes," she said, turning it up even more. "This is Nana's favorite song."

A rap song played on the radio. "Nana is hard of hearing."

Sadie stuck out her tongue. "Stop deflecting, old man."

"When did you start using that term?" Apparently, all those therapy sessions were making their way into her vocabulary.

"Am I wrong?" She turned off the radio. "You like Miss Johnson."

"Look, Sadie, I know you think you know, but you really don't, okay?" He didn't want to talk about this make-believe crush any longer. It was nonsense.

"Whatever." Sadie made that face like she was totally going to keep bringing it up and believing what she said.

Maybe the girl was a fortune teller because ever since she started bringing it up, he couldn't stop thinking of the beautiful newcomer. Here was this gorgeous woman who knew exactly what he needed in his life at the exact right time, yet she couldn't stand him. Ever since the first time she'd come into the market, she'd told him what he was doing wrong. Wrong wine, wrong shelving organization, wrong, wrong, wrong.

He didn't like her. She irritated him. But he needed her help, because whether or not he liked to admit it, she knew what she was doing. But beyond that, she was a pain in the rear. Well, except for Sadie. She had been really helpful with Sadie.

"You're going to school," he said, ending the conversation.

After he dropped her off, he walked into the market to see his father taking a picture in front of the mural.

They're here," Remy said, ushering him through the store to the camera crew.

"Are you Colby St. Germain?" a woman asked him, holding out her hand. She wore a dress suit with higher heels than he'd ever seen in Blueberry Bay.

"Yes," he said, looking around the store.

"I'm Debra Fox from Channel Five News," she said, shaking his hand. "Do you mind if we talk to you about the Jacob O'Neill mural you discovered?"

He glanced over at Remy, his heart beating a hundred miles a minute. He didn't want to talk into the camera that was suddenly in his face. He cleared his throat. "Actually, it was one of our employees who discovered it, and we couldn't have been more pleased to see our local hero's work in our market."

He hoped he sounded like he knew what he was talking about. Remy hadn't mentioned he'd have to talk.

"Um, I wasn't prepared to be on camera," he said.

"You look fine," the reporter said, but he noticed more paint on her face than Jacob's mural. "Just a few words about the piece."

"It's very significant to Jacob's history," Remy said, stepping next to Colby. The reporter turned towards her, moving her attention away from Colby, which he was grateful for. "He fished this harbor and supplied this market with his lobster. The mural represents community and togetherness. It represents the peace and tranquility the village offers but also shows all the hard work it took to get here."

Colby listened in awe as Remy continued talking about the significance of all the different parts of Jacob's painting. He hadn't even thought about the significance of Jacob himself being a fisherman, as well as, the artist of the mural. He looked at his father, who was talking to the cameraman, pointing out parts of the mural. The village of Blueberry Bay had been encapsulated in the painting. How could they have covered it up for cocktail sauce all these years?

"The market is the heart of what this town represents," Remy continued on to the reporter. "It's only fitting that this beautiful piece of artwork is in the place where you can get the freshest lobster Maine has to offer. You'll find no better or friendlier place."

"While admiring Jacob O'Neill's only mural," Colby added.

Debra Fox turned to the cameraman and started directing the shots. Emil had been the first shot, then Lucy and Emil, then Colby. The whole thing was a lot shorter than Colby had expected when he'd first heard about the news crew coming last night. He was still in shock about the whole thing.

After they took all their photos, asked all their questions, the reporter finished by telling the people of Boston to take a weekend getaway to Blueberry Bay and check out Harbor Market.

When it was all over, Debra Fox turned to Remy and said, "Thanks so much for the tip."

"Anytime," Remy said, turning the sign to open.

The crew began cleaning up all their equipment and Colby joined Remy behind the counter, watching them pack up.

"How'd you get the news to cover our little market?" He couldn't believe it. The free publicity could be a huge boost for the market.

"I called them up and told them about Jacob's newly discovered mural," she said, watching as customers came in and asked for photos with Debra Fox.

"That's really above your pay grade," he said, impressed she'd even think to do something like this for them.

"What better way to get the attention of wealthy art fanatics' who love to spend money on expensive fish?" She shrugged her shoulders like it was no big deal.

But it was a very big deal.

As Remy walked over to the reporter and Emil, he realized two very important things.

Sadie was never going to forgive him for not being in the shot.

And that his niece must have psychic powers, because as Remy had talked to the reporter about the mural with confidence and ease, he couldn't keep his eyes off her. He was falling for the beautiful woman.

"We'll have to come up during that festival you were talking about," the producer said.

"It's called the Blueberry Festival, but it's in August," Remy informed them.

"There's the Blessing of the Fleet," Colby said quickly. "Harbor Market sponsors it every year."

"That's perfect for this kind of segment!" Debra said, pointing her index finger at him.

They had sponsored it for over fifty years, a tradition Emil refused to stop even though they didn't have it in the budget, but maybe they could get attention on it and bring in more business.

"The Blessing of the Fleet would be perfect," Remy said, turning to Colby.

Colby nodded. "It's a tradition in a lot of fishing towns. It's to bless the season with good fortune. It takes place right out front in the town square. We supply the lobster."

Emil smiled behind the reporter, and Colby felt a shot of pride being able to stand there and share what they do for their town.

"Thanks again for doing all this," Colby said to Remy when she came in from saying goodbye to Debra Fox.

"I just made a call," she said. That's all."

She shrugged, then without offering any more, she walked away.

He watched her go back behind the counter. He didn't know much about this woman, but he did know her talents were wasted working behind a cash register.

When he walked up to her to tell her so, he noticed her hands were shaking, and he didn't know what, but something had happened since the time she'd left.

"What's wrong?" he asked.

She shook her head, her eyes darting in another direction. "It's nothing."

But he could tell it was more than just nothing.

"Did she say something to you?" He looked out the window to see the news van pulling away.

"No. I mean, not really." She sighed heavily. "She told me about something."

"What was it about?" he asked, not dropping it. She was visibly upset.

She cast her eyes down. "My ex is engaged."

His hand went straight to her shaking ones, and he gently placed it on top. "Are you okay?"

"I'm not upset about the engagement," she said quickly, as if defending herself.

"I'd be upset," he said.

"I'm not upset he moved on," she said. "It's just that he made a statement about starting a family."

She stared out the window, and he saw moisture build up in her eyes, but she didn't cry. She held up her chin as though fighting it back.

"And that cut a little," she said. "Because I wasn't able to start my own family…" She let out a sad laugh. "He did tell me that I was replaceable."

Colby didn't ask about people and their choice to have children. He of all people understood how difficult the decision was to have a family. Melanie had said she wanted children at some point, but she'd wanted to travel and work. She hadn't wanted to be "locked down" with kids. She hadn't even wanted to get pets for the same reason. She had loved the idea of him fishing. He could choose his hours, go where they'd wanted to go, and not answer to anyone.

But when Brynn had taken off and the state had stepped in with Sadie, what was he supposed to do? Leave his niece and family behind in their darkest hour?

He could blame the destruction of his marriage on Brynn's neglect, but Melanie and his marriage had been over long before that. She had worked longer hours, traveled farther and for longer stretches. When she'd been home, she had never wanted to be there, finding excuses to leave.

When she had skipped his birthday, their anniversary, and Christmas, he'd known things between them were fragile at best. It came as no surprise when she just hadn't come home one day.

When he'd looked in her closet after she had called and told him she wanted to end their marriage, almost all of her belongings were already gone. How he hadn't noticed the problems until Brynn blew them out of the dark was beyond him.

Sadie had been eight when Brynn had first left, then nine, then ten. It had been harder to watch Brynn than it had been to take care of Sadie.

Then Sadie had started a fire in his parents' kitchen, and the state had stepped in again. That had been when he'd moved in and when Melanie had filed for divorce.

Now he was stuck like an anchor, while Melanie was free as a bird, traveling the world like she'd always wanted. Her social media had been filled with solo traveling and new journeys and hashtags reading #mybestlife!

Not that he would change a thing. Well, maybe he'd change a few things. He still didn't want to run a market, he still didn't want to live with his parents, and he still wanted to have a family and be married. But he'd never regret his decision to help his family and move into the house to raise Sadie and let go of Melanie's dreams.

"My wife left me when I got custody of Sadie," he blurted out. He didn't even bother to see if there were customers close by. It didn't matter. Everyone in town knew about it. Those Queens must've told her by now.

"I'm sorry," she said, and they both stood in silence for a moment before she said, "But she did you a favor."

He cocked his head, eager to hear her answer. "How's that?"

"Because you get to raise that amazing little girl," she said, blinking at him.

Her words hit him like a truth bomb. He just wished Melanie would've stayed. He didn't know how to explain periods and bras and where to shave. He needed help. His parents were older, his mother's health deteriorating with the stress of not knowing where her daughter was or if she was alive. Emil pretended to save the market by working all the time but sat in his office hiding from the world.

"But you obviously need a lot of help." She smiled, and he could tell she was joking.

He lifted the side of his mouth.

"Is that a smile?" she asked.

"I can do it from time to time," he said.

She laughed. "You should do it more often. You look nice when you do."

"Nice?" He laughed again. "Gee, thanks."

But the compliment made his heart skip a beat, and he got that feeling again. The one he wanted to pound down and forget.

"Like someone wanting to help the customer find a local wine," she said, referring to their first interaction.

"Oh my god, you were such a snob about it, though," he said, ready to argue the reason he had been so moody.

"You should've lost me as a customer," she said.

"As I recall, Emil gave you free lobsters that day." He remembered losing his mind as his father handed over six perfect over-a-pound lobsters for just being related to Jacob O'Neill.

Remy lifted her chin in the air and crossed her arms. "I may recall something like that."

He rolled his eyes, but he wasn't annoyed. He was eager to keep playing along with her. This Remy, the one who was able to joke about herself and loosen up, was the Remy he couldn't stop staring at or thinking about.

She swept her hair behind her and over one shoulder, and the fragrance of her shampoo sent electric waves running through his body.

"Hello!" a voice called from the back.

From the office, Bridgette came out, dangling a baby carrier on her arm.

Remy's mouth dropped open, and she immediately squealed in delight. "I want to see the baby!" Remy squirted hand sanitizer into her hands and rubbed furiously as she ran around the counter and straight to Bridgette. "May I see her?"

Remy didn't get close like the other women who came around the baby. Most people just started touching and getting into Camden's face, saying all kinds of weird things to make the baby notice them.

"She just woke from a nap, so she'll probably have a dirty diaper," Bridgette said.

"Let me take care of it," Remy said, pulling back her sleeves, which Colby thought seemed very expensive.

"Ah, yes, please." Bridgette set the baby carrier onto the counter and unstrapped a very tiny Camden out of her seat.

Colby couldn't believe his baby sister was a mother, but there she was pulling a baby the size of a five-pound lobster out of a baby carrier. And it was bald.

Maybe it was a good thing he didn't have kids.

"Why is her head thumping?" Sadie asked.

Bridgette carefully placed the baby on Remy's shoulder, who

stretched and smacked her tiny little lips together. "It's her soft spot."

"Looks like a hole," Colby said, looking at Camden's round head.

"It's basically a hole at this point," Bridgette said.

"Why does she have that?" Sadie asked.

"Because the baby needed to get out of my body," Bridgette said matter-of-factly.

"Oh," Sadie said, backing away from the baby. "Ouch."

"Yeah," Bridgette said, as Colby became increasingly uncomfortable.

"When's Tim able to come back home?" Colby asked, knowing his sister's husband, who had been deployed out at sea, would still have weeks before he'd be able to see his newborn child. The sacrifices the men and women gave to their country made what Colby was doing seem like nothing.

"Two weeks," Bridgette said, making faces at the baby.

Oh course, he would take care of his sister when her husband was away. Of course, he'd take legal guardianship of his niece when his other sister took off. Of course, he'd work at the market to save his parents. What else could he do? Take off like Melanie? Run away like Brynn?

"You must miss him," Remy said to Bridget.

"Yes, but my mom and dad take such good care of us." Bridgette passed baby Camden into Remy's arms. "And Uncle Colby here is such a huge help."

Colby couldn't help but watch Remy snuggle the baby into her arms.

"She feels clean, so enjoy," Bridgette said.

"What's the best part?" Remy asked, swaying her and the baby back and forth like a natural.

"Of motherhood?" Bridgette asked and looked up at the ceiling. "Everything except sleeping. She's a good baby, but it's hard waking up all the time and getting just a few minutes of sleep here and there. Everyone tries to help when they can, but it's a lot of work no matter how you look at it."

"Sleep is a wonderful thing," Remy agreed.

"I know they say it goes by fast, so I'm trying to savor every moment." Bridgette took Camden's socked foot in her hand and smelled it. "Even her feet are delicious."

Bridgette stayed and talked for a while before Camden got fussy.

"I better go feed her." Bridgette grabbed her diaper bag and carrier.

Remy passed the baby back to Bridgette, then said, "You know, if you ever need anyone to babysit, I'd love to help."

"Seriously? I might take you up on that," Bridgette said.

"I love babies." Remy played with Camden's little hand. "It's been a long time since I've been around one."

Colby felt a sadness radiating out of her comment and it made him walk away before he said something stupid or weirded her out. But it made him want to break whoever had broken Remy's heart.

After Bridgette took the baby back home for a nap, he decided to listen to his wise-beyond-her-years niece and just ask Remy out. Just go for it. He'd start by asking about the move and if she needed anything, then maybe ask her if he could make her dinner. Or maybe take her somewhere. But where in Blueberry Bay could he take her? And if he did take her out in Blueberry Bay, everyone and their mother would be talking about it. He'd have to take her somewhere out of town. Then things would just get even more complicated.

He just wouldn't ask.

"Everything okay?" Remy asked as he walked out into the front of the store.

He waved at her. "Yeah, everything's fine."

"You're so lucky to have such a large family," Remy said. "I always wanted a big family. Your dad told me there's six of you. I can't even imagine."

"It's a lot." Colby found it to be a curse and a blessing. "Sometimes all you want is privacy, some space, and to be alone. But you can't. But then, you have your own live-in basketball team, so it worked out."

"I always thought I'd have at least three, but I wanted to try for four," Remy said, then she smiled the saddest smile Colby had ever seen.

"Would you believe that Sadie told me about the birds and the bees so that I could"—he held up his fingers to air quote— "hurry up and have a baby?"

He still couldn't believe the conversation had happened in the waiting room at the orthodontist's office.

An explosion of laughter came out of Remy, and it immediately made him laugh. "That's a riot. She did not."

"While getting her braces tightened," he added. "Dr. Brandt chimed in."

This got her rolling in laughter. "I could actually see her doing that."

As Remy continued to giggle about Sadie's sex talk, he decided to go for it. He'd ask her out. What did he have to lose at that point? She already thought he was crazy, and maybe he was, but he swore she might be feeling something like he did.

"So, I was thinking that when you move in, I could—"

"Remy!" a voice called out from the front of the store. Roland Foster crossed the store in rapid succession and stood next to her before Colby could get another word out.

"Roland." She looked down at her phone and waved. "I have about five minutes left of my shift, and I can leave then."

"Great, I'll wait outside over at the park," he said, jabbing his thumb in the direction.

"No need," Colby said, his heart plummeting like an anchor. "You can take off now if you want."

"Really?" Remy started to untie her apron. She looked at Roland. "I guess I can leave now."

Colby so badly wanted to know more and ask questions.

What were they doing together? Where did they plan to go? Had Roland broken through Remy's hard exterior and gotten her to agree to a date? He needed to get out of his head.

"Do you think we could meet tomorrow at the house?" Remy asked Colby. "Go through some of the things you want to put into storage?"

"I'll be there." Colby silently thanked the heavens above that he hadn't asked Remy out. He had no business asking a woman like her on a date. She had seriously rich men willing to court her for weeks. She was talented and confident and fun. And man, was she smart and sexy.

Was he an idiot for not asking her out, or had he saved himself from a world of embarrassment?

"Is this your landlord?" Roland asked.

"Yes, he's the one." Remy tilted her head as she kept her glance on Roland.

Or was there really something happening between them?

"Did you tell him about all the things that needed to be worked on?" Roland asked.

Her mouth dropped open as though she were about to answer, but Colby spoke before she could. "Send it in a text so I'll remember."

He pretended to move on to a customer and help them, trying not to look as she left with the rich guy.

What was he doing? He needed to get it together. She clearly didn't have any sort of feelings for him other than being her new landlord.

CHAPTER 19

$\mathcal{R}$emy asked Kyle, Quinn's son, and a couple of his friends to move some of the furniture she had stored in the barn over the winter and bring it to the new house.

When they arrived, Meredith and Ginny had already begun cleaning inside, while Gordon and Quinn and Colby walked around the house, making sure all the faucets and light fixtures and appliances worked correctly.

"Colby, you've done a really nice job with the place," Quinn said, closing the back door. "I remember when this was your grandmother's house."

Remy loved it. Yes, it was small and needed a lot of cosmetic updates, but Quinn was right. The old house had been nicely renovated. The original woodwork had been beautifully restored. She couldn't believe her good fortune.

She nodded in agreement. "These traditional New England homes built in seaside towns back in the day just have a different kind of character than the houses built today."

"It's adorable, Remy," Meredith said. "It reminds me of a gingerbread house."

The decorative trim along the roofline did make the house

feel a little gingerbready. "I don't think I could've asked for a better place to start my new chapter."

Colby should be very proud of his accomplishments. What a shame he couldn't stay there.

"Can I paint?" Remy asked. "I'll pay for it."

"Sure," Colby said. "Just nothing crazy, like fluorescent yellow."

The corner of Remy's mouth perked up. "Just a shade of fuchsia."

"You want to paint it pink?" Colby asked, his face twisted at the thought.

Remy let out a laugh, and it made Colby relax. "No, I'm kidding. Just soft shades of gray and white."

"Let me pay for it and help paint," he said. "I should probably refresh the place for you anyway. Isn't that what a landlord should do?"

She shook her head. "That's really not necessary."

"I'd like to," he said, his eyes catching hers, and gratitude flowed through her. "You can take it as a thank you for everything you've done."

Remy's heart filled with happiness.

"For what?" Remy didn't know why he needed to thank her. "I should be thanking you."

Colby laughed at this. "Seriously, we've made a huge profit since all your changes. We have more customer interactions, more people coming to see the mural and buying the lobster, and then all the other things you suggested on their way to the register. We've never seen such sales during the offseason. We've almost doubled what we made last year at this time."

"Really?" Remy didn't doubt they'd get more business, but double? "Wow."

Meredith's eyebrow lifted. "You redesigned their store?"

Remy shrugged, not sure what to say. "I just suggested some things."

"More than just suggested—completely changed the way of

business at the market," Colby said, and when no one else was looking, Colby gave her a nod, and a feeling grew inside her. A feeling of happiness as she stood around the house as her family and Colby talked about the space.

"Sadie would love to help paint, too," Colby said.

"Have her come by this weekend," Remy said, counting the days. She'd have enough time to wash down the walls and get everything taped.

"Sounds great," Colby said, stuffing his hands into his pockets. "Is there anything else you need from me today?"

She looked around the space, joy filling her soul. "Nope, I'm good."

Remy took the whole weekend off to move in. After Kyle and his friends moved the furniture inside the house, Meredith and Remy spent the day organizing the downstairs and making Remy's bed up.

"Do you want me to spend the night?" Meredith asked. Her sister would always act like a second mother, and Remy hadn't ever been grateful until recently.

"I'm good," Remy said, looking forward to having the whole house to herself. "You can always send Dad over here if you need some alone time."

"He's always at Ginny's," Meredith said. "I'm going to be lonely at the house now."

Remy didn't believe it. She'd have Quinn there all the time. And Meredith deserved every second she spent with a man she adored.

"Hey, how did dinner go with Roland the other night?" Meredith asked, hoping this would be the right guy for Remy.

Remy thought about the night. When she'd taken out her drawings for her design ideas, Roland had told her he didn't want to discuss business during dinner, and when dessert had come, he'd suggested meeting another time to talk about it. By the end of the night, Remy decided not to bother asking about the design anymore.

"Eh," Remy said, wiping down the banister. "He's a little...I don't know."

She couldn't put her finger on it. Something about him didn't feel right.

By the time Meredith took off, the house had all the furniture Remy owned placed where she wanted it for now, a freshly made bed, a television set up, but no internet yet. She pulled out her phone and turned on some music. She grabbed a lighter and began lighting the few candles she had. She wanted to place them around the house as the sun began to set and take a tour of her new home.

But as she put a candle in the dining room, she heard a knock on the back door. She looked at the time. It was seven at night.

She walked to the door and saw Colby standing there. "Colby? What are you doing here?"

He held up a wicker basket that had a bottle of white wine sticking out of it. She recognized the brand right away. It was what she had suggested the first time she'd walked into the market. "I wanted to bring you a housewarming gift."

She hadn't seen that brand carried anywhere in Maine. "Where did you find it?"

He laughed. "I ordered a bunch for the market." He then handed over the basket to her. "I made my own."

She backed up into the house. "Come in."

She walked right over to the butcher block and placed the basket on top. She pulled out the wine, which was chilled, a thermos, a loaf of bread, oyster crackers, a container with salad written across it, and a package of cookies.

"I call it 'A Maine Lunch for the Beach,'" he said. "My own clam chowder recipe with a loaf of bread from the bakery, blueberry jam from the Queen Bees, a salad that will be all locally grown, along with a treat."

"This is brilliant," she said.

"I'll use those refrigerators that we have and set it up for a create-your-own-basket, take-out situation," he said, staring straight into her eyes, but it felt like he was staring right into her heart. "What do you think?"

Her knees wobbled. The way he looked at her, the way that he had taken her ideas and thought they were good, made her more attracted to him than ever at that moment.

"It's a perfect idea," Remy said, practically breathless.

Colby smiled. "I thought you'd like it."

"Would you like to stay for a glass of wine?" she asked, secretly hoping he'd say yes.

He looked at his watch. "I would really like that, but I need to pick Sadie up from a dance."

This made her grin in delight. "She's at a dance tonight? I used to love dances."

"She'll love telling you all about it," he said. "She's on the student council and decorated for it. I had to hear about it for weeks."

Remy laughed. "She's a lovely young lady. You've done a really great job with her."

Colby's eyes locked onto hers. It was a look she couldn't explain but understood completely. They kept the stare, not speaking, not needing to say what was happening between them.

"Come with me to pick her up," he said.

A rush of adrenaline washed through her body. "I'd love to."

She blew out the candles but left all the lights on. She wanted to drive back with *her* new house aglow.

CHAPTER 20

*C*olby couldn't help but watch Remy's reaction when Sadie came out of the dance in her too-small, too-revealing dress.

"She looks adorable!" Remy squealed from the passenger seat.

"Hey, Ms. Johnson," Sadie said, getting into the back seat of Colby's truck. "What are you doing with Uncle Colby? Are you two on a date?"

"No, not a date," Remy answered quickly.

"He wants to ask you," Sadie said back.

"Geez, Sadie, that's not appropriate," he said, wishing he could crawl underneath his truck and disappear. What was his niece doing to him?

"Well, I'm sure your uncle is being completely professional," Remy said, but he noted she didn't scoff at the idea. In fact, she didn't deter him.

"Remy wanted to see what a dance looks like these days," Colby said, knowing full well Sadie would forget being a matchmaker the second she started talking about how she and the others in student council chose the theme for this year's spring dance.

"It took six weeks for us to come up with Spring Fling," Sadie said, all serious.

Remy let out a laugh so light and bright and cheery, Colby swore the moon glowed brighter.

"Do you want to go inside and see?" Sadie asked. "It's really beautiful."

"The Queen Bees even helped," Colby said.

"They did?" Remy had skipped a few meetings due to being so busy with work.

"Uncle Colby, park the truck!" Sadie ordered. She swung her door open before he put the truck into park. "Let me show you everything we did."

Remy jumped out and followed Sadie into the gymnasium entrance. A pastel balloon archway greeted them as they walked into the gym. With the lights dimmed and strobe lights still moving around, Remy saw only a few adults left cleaning up.

"Sadie, did you forget something?" a bald man asked.

"No, I just wanted to show my uncle's special friend what the dance looked like." Sadie pulled Remy by the hand farther into the gym.

"Oh, Sadie!" Remy twirled in a circle. "It's beautiful."

Yellow daffodils, pink tulips, and blue hyacinth sat in pots on the tables and scattered throughout the room. The tables had white tablecloths and balloons floating above. Decorations were set up on the walls and throughout the bleachers.

"We had a selfie station here." Sadie pointed to a little area set up with gardening tools and hats. "Everyone loved taking the pictures with all the silly hats." She dragged Remy even deeper into the gym. "This is where we had a build-your-own-sundae station."

"This turned out fantastic," Remy said, clearly impressed.

"The boys even had a dodgeball tournament in the smaller gym over there." Sadie gestured with her chin to the double doors.

"You and your friends did a great job," Colby said to Sadie, equally impressed.

"Mr. St. Germain!" a woman said from the punch bowl. "Do you have a moment?"

Sadie pulled Remy to the other side of the gym, and Colby cut away to the teacher.

"Sure," he said.

"Didn't Sadie do a nice job with the decorations?" the teacher commented.

"Yes, she did." Colby turned his head to check it out one more time.

"I wanted to talk to you about some concerns I have with Sadie."

The happiness bubble he had walked into the gym with suddenly burst. "What kind of concerns?"

"She can be overly bossy when it comes to the other kids, and when she doesn't get her way, she tends to break down and be really hard on herself."

Colby knew Sadie had some anger issues. Her therapist said her obsessive-compulsive behavior was a defensive mechanism used to cope with her feelings that she's lost control.

"Sadie's going through a lot," he reminded the teacher. "She has a hard time with relationships."

"Yes, but she also has to learn to control her behavior, otherwise she's going to lose those friends." The teacher made a face of sympathy, and it broke Colby's heart. Because she was right. Sadie didn't keep friends around. She usually pushed them away, or they went running because of her demands.

He looked over at Sadie, pulling Remy's hand to the bathroom. "I'll talk to her and bring this up with her therapist."

"That would be great," the teacher said. "She's a brilliant young lady but needs a little bit of help with her social skills."

"Sure," he said, waiting for the girls to come back out of the bathroom.

When Sadie and Remy came out, he noticed they had applied

the same color lipstick, and he smiled at the two giggling about something.

"What's so funny?" he asked, wishing he wasn't thinking about how much he liked hanging out with Remy.

"Oh, it's nothing," Sadie said in a fit of giggles.

He looked at Remy, who shrugged. "I don't know."

But the two laughed together, knowing exactly what they were laughing about, and he knew he was in too deep to change direction now. Hopefully rich guy liked a little competition, because he was going to ask Remy out tonight.

Or at least that's what he had planned until Sadie blocked every chance he had to ask her. She talked and talked and talked about the dance until Remy said goodbye and closed the truck door.

"Why didn't you ask her out?" Sadie asked.

"Because you wouldn't stop talking," he said back.

"I didn't talk that much," she said, playing with the window. "What did Mrs. Kneeland want?"

So, she had seen her teacher talk to him. "She told me you were getting upset with your friends about planning the dance."

"They had stupid ideas," she said, as though that was enough to treat someone badly.

"You know, there are enough jerks in the world," Colby said. "You don't want to be one of them, right?"

She looked at Colby like he had two heads. "They wanted to do a scary movie theme for a middle school dance. What kind of props can you do with that kind of theme when we can't even draw weapons in school? It would have been totally lame."

"Come on, Sadie, you're going to lose your friends if you treat them poorly," he said.

"You deal with Lily Patterson and tell me you don't have to raise your voice," she argued. "Besides, I don't even want them as my friends. I have you guys."

"But we're old." He closed his eyes. He loved the fact that his niece considered him worthy enough to spend time with, but to be her only friend couldn't be healthy.

He would ask Remy to talk to her. He bet she'd know what to do.

He looked at Sadie. That girl was a psychic.

"What?"

"I think you're right," he said, driving into the garage. "I'm going to ask her out."

Sadie threw her arms up into the air. "Yeah!"

"But only if you have a sleepover," he said.

Her smile dropped as fast as her arms to her side. "What?"

"You have to invite three friends over for a sleepover." Colby didn't know what he was doing, but he had to do something. Sadie couldn't have a forty-year-old man be her best friend.

"Fine." She started texting as they got out of the truck.

Colby could hear a baby crying inside. He silently groaned, exhausted from the day, but he put his game face on as soon as he opened the door.

"Thank goodness you're home," Bridgette said, passing him baby Camden. "I have throw up all over me."

"Take your time," he told his baby sister, who didn't even hear his response, as she was already heading upstairs.

"Done." Sadie held out her phone and showed a group text with phrases like, *I can make it* and *Yes!* followed by various emojis. "Now you have to ask her."

Colby swayed back and forth with Camden in his arms, who he swore was staring right back at him. How long did it take for babies to recognize faces and understand facial expressions? He swore Camden was the smartest baby already.

"I can't tonight, but I will tomorrow after her shift so it's not awkward all day," he promised.

"If you don't ask by the time I have to go to practice, I'm going to ask her for you," Sadie said, going up the stairs.

"Are you going to bed?" he asked her, hoping she'd help with the baby.

"I have to take a shower before bed," Sadie reminded him.

"Right," he said. He looked for his parents. His mother would be out playing bridge with the girls, and his father would be at the local tavern with all his fishing buddies.

He thought about texting Remy, telling her to come smell the baby. He had seen her sniff Camden's head the whole time she'd held her at the market.

He inhaled Camden's head. It was strange how wonderful a baby smells.

"We already love you to pieces," he whispered in the baby's ear. "You're already so smart, and one day you can be anything you want to be."

He looked down at his baby niece, wondering what she'd be like at thirteen.

"Uncle Colby will always take care of you." He meant it, too. This child would be forever taken care of as long as he lived.

A little part of him ached at the idea that he didn't have his own family to share this moment with. He would love to have someone by his side as he held his niece. He wanted to share his life with someone, not change it. He wouldn't change a thing. Not even letting go of Melanie.

He went to the fridge, holding Camden like a football, and grabbed a beer, but then he stopped himself when he saw an open bottle of wine Remy always raved about. After pulling it out and setting it onto the counter, he pulled the cork out and sniffed the top. He expected a bitter smell like with other white wines he'd tried, but this one had a sweet fragrance almost like a flower. From the cabinet above, he took out a wineglass and poured himself some.

He took a sip, ready for his jaw to clench from its bitterness, but instead the wine glided down his throat smoothly. It was good. Really good.

He took another sip and laughed.

"What's so funny?" Bridgette asked, walking back into the room.

"Wow, that's the fastest shower I've ever seen," he said.

"Well, when you're a mother, you have to be quick about everything," she said with absolute pride across her face. "And Sadie was banging on the door the whole time."

Colby had to admit that motherhood made his sister even more beautiful than before. "You're a great mother."

"Thanks, Colb," she said. "Want me to take her?"

He shook his head. "I've got her. Why don't you have this wine and relax."

Bridgette swept her arms around his waist and kissed his cheek. "I love you."

She left before he could say anything back, swiping the glass of wine out of his hands, and went into the family room. With a click of a button, she turned on the television.

"There's a hockey game on," he said into the family room.

When he walked in, Bridgette was watching a reality show about rich housewives.

"Want to hang out in the kitchen and watch grown men beat each other up?" he asked baby Camden.

He walked back into the kitchen and sat down at the table with his niece in his arms. His went back to earlier in the day, back to Remy's laugh, and back to his feelings growing. There was no question now that he was starting to fall for her.

"How did this even happen?" he asked the baby. "Sheesh."

CHAPTER 21

*R*emy stood in her new bathroom and waited for the tub to fill. She looked at her reflection in the mirror. She almost didn't recognize herself. Over the years, she had always gone all out on her looks. The women she'd hung around started plastic surgery young. Botox to fill in little hairline wrinkles that only the woman herself could see. Heavy make-up that covered any imperfections. Hair styled perfectly and in place. Clothes and shoes were only high fashion, not high function.

Now in Blueberry Bay, Remy had stopped wearing a lot of make-up, if any. When she worked, she put on mascara and lipstick. Maybe a little eyeshadow. Even if she wanted to, she couldn't afford the kind or amount of make-up she'd used back when she was married to Joe.

She didn't miss the make-up or the lifestyle. She missed none of it, not even Joe.

As the tub filled, she sat on the edge and wrote in her journal.

She wrote about the move and the people who had helped her. She wrote about the kindness Colby had shared by allowing her to stay in the house. She wrote about the news station coming to film a story about the mural. She wrote about the new changes and success of the market. She wrote about Sadie showing her around the dance. She wrote about Colby's basket and how kind he turned out to be.

She picked up her pen and tapped it against the page, her thoughts once again circling back to Colby.

With at least a dozen or so candles lit, she slowly lowered herself into the clawfoot tub. She closed her eyes, in complete bliss at the moment. She'd done it. She had started her journey. Now it was on an upward from here. She would make her dreams come true.

She picked up her glass of wine from the bath tray she'd taken from her old house and took a long sip. She held up her glass.

"To a new journey," she said aloud, hoping somewhere her mother was listening. *"Vers un nouveau voyage."*

Her mother had spoken fluent French, and she had often spoken the language to her and her sister. It turned out to be something Joe had admired about her. Remy didn't speak it very well, if correctly, but enough to buy a loaf of bread and get around in Paris.

But now in Blueberry Bay, it had become extremely helpful. Lindy loved how she could talk to all the French-Canadians that came through the village. At the market, she could speak on the phone with their suppliers in Quebec.

Her thoughts went back to Colby. She swore something was happening between them, and if Sadie hadn't been leaning between them over the console from the back and talking the whole time before he'd dropped Remy off, he might have been in less of a rush to say goodbye.

But Colby liked her. That much, Sadie had said. But Remy thought his eyes said it too. She'd sworn he was going to ask her out, and if he had, she would have said yes. But what if he thought it would be completely inappropriate to ask out an employee?

After an hour of reading and her eyes getting tired, Remy got out of the bath and noticed a text message from Roland. She almost didn't respond but thought better. He was still her client, and she didn't want to be unprofessional.

She read the text. He wanted to have another dinner to go over her plans.

She texted back. **Sounds great.** But noticed his invitation to dinner was vague—no time, no day.

When Remy went to bed that night, she did one more walk through the house, looking in every cabinet and drawer, planning out the way she wanted to decorate and arrange her things. Changes she would make if she could. Mostly, she admired the space. If the house went up on the market, someone like Roland might come along and tear it down, never even bothering to see the beauty in the house.

What had been on Roland's property before he'd built his house? A fisherman's house like this one? Or a blueberry field? She certainly couldn't look down on him for what he had done. Joe had done the same things for most of his houses.

Gotten rid of whatever stood in his way.

After her last walk through, she pulled the covers over herself and listened to the silence. Faintly, just barely, she could hear the soft rhythm of the ocean.

And Remy fell asleep like a baby.

And suddenly woke up the next morning to her phone ringing her alarm.

She looked at the time.

"Eight o'clock!" She jumped out of bed. She was late for her shift at the market.

She hurried to get dressed, then brushed her teeth and hair. She skipped her coffee and breakfast, running out the door and to her car.

She hadn't slept that heavily in years. Since she was a kid. And it felt good. She felt well and rested. She rubbed her cheeks to get some color and drove as fast as she could to work.

"Hey," Colby said, either not noticing or not caring she was ten minutes late.

"I'm sorry I'm late," she said. "I overslept."

He shook his head. "No problem."

Colby walked away, and Remy watched as he left. She couldn't exactly put her finger on it, but he was acting weird.

Maybe she was wrong about last night. Maybe she had made him uncomfortable and now he didn't know how to act around her.

She panicked for a second that she had done something to cross the line. She flashed through the moments of the other day in rapid succession. Nothing came to mind.

Stop getting in your head, she thought to herself. She went behind the counter, put on her apron, and set her purse under the shelf.

"Remy! Just the person I was talking about," Emil said, coming out from the back. "How's the house?"

"It's absolutely perfect," she said, thinking about her night's sleep. She wished she had woken to the alarm she'd set to see the sunrise on her new porch. Oh well, she had plenty of time to do that now.

"My bedroom as a little boy was the attic," he said. "I used to pretend I was a king in a castle with my fleet of ships below."

Remy smiled at the idea that the lobster boats that anchored in Blueberry Bay were his kingdom. She imagined a little boy standing at the window with a wooden sword and a plastic gold crown. "How sweet was that?"

"I had a great childhood growing up there," he said. "I hope you love living there as much as I did."

"I know I will," she said. "I love it already."

She did. She couldn't wait to get home. She loved her sister, but she wanted her own space. A place where she felt she could be anywhere she wanted without permission. Not that Meredith made her feel like she had to have permission, but the fact remained—Jacob's cottage was Meredith's inheritance, not Remy's.

She thought about the sewing room Meredith had at her

house. She'd like to do the same, but in the attic. She loved sewing and she could start making projects for the Queen Bees, maybe even make curtains and reupholster some furniture. Maybe even make some of the drapery for Roland once he chose his colors and design.

On her lunch break, she noticed Colby was missing, and she took her sandwich to the park with her sketch pad. The spring weather had warmed up enough to sit outside without a coat, and Remy wanted to take full advantage of it. She missed the sun.

She also started to enjoy having lunch by her mother's statue. Almost like a lunch date with her. She sat on the bench across from it and had a silent, private conversation with Jacqueline the mermaid.

But as she came around the bright yellow forsythia bushes, she saw Sadie sitting on her bench.

"Fancy meeting you here," Remy said to the young girl whose eyes were focused on her phone.

But when Remy got closer, she noticed Sadie was crying.

"Sadie." She instantly sat down. "What's the matter?"

Sadie dropped her phone onto the ground and covered her face. Remy bent over to pick the phone up and saw a text message.

My mom says I can't sleep over anymore.

Y? Sadie asked back.

Because she says your mom's a criminal.

"Oh, Sadie." Remy wrapped her arms around the girl instantly. "That's not right. That mother is not being kind to you."

This made Sadie cry hard; thick, heavy heaves roared from her chest. The sound alone made Remy's eyes swell with tears. She knew that kind of pain. The pain of not having a mother.

She held Sadie, rocking her back and forth like she did with her nieces and nephew. She held Sadie as though she were her own and held her until Sadie moved away.

Sadie wiped her face with her hands as Remy dug into her purse for tissues. "Here."

Sadie took the tissues and blew her nose. "Thank you."

"You want to talk about it?" Remy asked. This was what she had learned growing up with a pediatrician—she had to listen to the patient before she could diagnose the problem.

Sadie shook her head.

She did what Gordon would do. She started asking questions.

"Who was that on the text?" Remy asked.

"Everyone in my group text," Sadie sniffled out. "Everyone knows about my mom now. They're going to tell everyone at school."

Remy could lie and tell her she was wrong, that the kids would be more mature, but she would be insulting Sadie's intelligence. They were going to spread this like wildfire and burn Sadie while doing it.

"That's not right," Remy said to her. "But don't let something like that break a strong young woman like yourself. This will pass and people will forget."

She scoffed. "No one forgets in this town."

"Do you know who that is?" Remy pointed to the statue of her mother. The mermaid was on a marble pedestal, eye level from where they sat.

Sadie shook her head, wiping her eyes with another tissue. "Who is it?"

"My mom," Remy said, looking at her beautiful mother and wishing she could actually be sitting here helping Sadie, too.

"That's your mom?" Sadie cocked her head at the bronze sculpture.

Remy looked at it with a new appreciation. "Well, at least the face. Beautiful, right?"

"Yes." Sadie nodded. "She is beautiful."

"The sculpture is beautiful, too," Remy said. "Don't you think?"

"Yes, it's really beautiful," Sadie agreed.

"It was made by my sister's father, who had to give up his

rights to her because he was unable to take care of her." Remy put her arm around Sadie's shoulder.

"The guy who made this is your father?" Sadie asked.

Remy shook her head. "No, he was my sister's father."

"Oh," she said, trying to piece together the family's history.

"But he couldn't take care of her because he drank and struggled with mental illness his whole life. Now the town celebrates him." Remy stared at the mermaid. "Sometimes the most beautiful things are created by the ones who are the most troubled. You are that beautiful creation your troubled mom created. Don't you ever let people make you feel otherwise."

Sadie looked at the statue. "My mom likes to cook when she's well."

Remy smiled. "My mom liked to cook too."

"Where is your mom now?" Sadie asked.

"She died a couple years ago," Remy said.

"I'm sorry." Sadie picked at her fingers. "I know what it's like to not have a mom."

Remy looked at her mother's face. The smile seemed so lifelike. "She was the best."

"Are you like her? Because I wish you were my mom," she said.

Remy's throat choked up, and all she could do was squeeze Sadie into her. "You have me as your friend, and that's a really special thing."

"Can I help paint your house?" Sadie said. "Uncle Colby said you were looking for someone to help paint."

"You know what?" Remy said. "I am."

Then an idea came to mind. "You know I haven't had a sleepover in a really long time. You think you might want to come over tonight and watch some movies and stay up late and eat a ton of candy with me?"

Sadie's eyes widened. "Yes, I do."

"We could do facials and pedis," Sadie said, thinking about all the things she'd done at sleepovers as a little girl.

"We should paint, too," Sadie said. "Maybe a mural of a mermaid!"

Remy thought about it. "That's not a terrible idea. I'd have to run it by your uncle of course, but I like it."

Sadie laughed. "My uncle will let you paint whatever you want. He's the reason why I had to ask those stupid girls to have a sleepover."

"What do you mean?" Remy asked.

"I was supposed to invite them over because he thinks I need help because the guidance counselor talked to him at the dance." Sadie said this in one long breath, so fast that Remy didn't understand what she was talking about.

"Your guidance counselor wants you to have a sleepover?" she asked, clarifying.

Sadie shook her head. "She thinks I'm bossy to kids and I push them away instead of being friendly."

Remy didn't have to be a guidance counselor to understand why Sadie might be like that, and the "friends" she had to choose from didn't seem all that great to begin with. "Well, maybe you could invite some other girls over?"

"There's barely any kids in this town," Sadie said.

"Sometimes, when we don't look around to see what's all there," she said. "We miss some things. I bet if you sat at a different table or joined a new club that sounds interesting, you'd find people more like yourself. Fun, creative, outgoing."

"You think kids will want to hang out with me knowing about my mom?" Sadie asked.

"Now you can assume everyone knows and not care about hiding the facts about your situation," Remy said. "You live with your wonderful family. That's pretty special and they love you and your mom so much, they'd do anything for you."

Sadie nodded. "My uncle would do anything for me." She scrunched up her nose. "Will you not tell him about the texts and stuff?"

This surprised Remy. "I don't like keeping secrets."

"He'll never forgive those girls for saying something so mean about my mom," Sadie said. "He's overly protective when it comes to me and my mom."

Sadie must have gone through similar situations before. "Okay, your secret is safe with me."

The two of them walked back to the market and walked in with Remy's arm still snuggly around Sadie's shoulder as they planned their night together.

"We have to have popcorn, and I love those Nerd gummy clusters," Remy said to Sadie.

"I do, too!" Sadie squealed in delight and no longer looked as though she had been crying at all.

"Just the people I was looking for," Colby said.

"You were?" Remy smiled as soon as she saw him, forgetting about his awkwardness earlier and just glad to see him again. She enjoyed seeing him, being around him, working with him. She enjoyed his dry sense of humor and watching him interact with his family. "Here we are."

"What were you guys doing?" he asked Sadie.

"We were planning out our sleepover," Sadie said back to him.

"You're having a sleepover with Remy?" He looked at Remy.

Remy lifted the corner of her mouth and looked at Sadie, who had a silent plea in her eyes to keep their secret.

"Sadie's friends had to cancel, and I thought it would be fun to have a sleepover at my new place," Remy said. "She can even sleep in her grandfather's old bedroom!"

Sadie's mouth dropped in excitement. "Did you hear that, Gramps? I'm sleeping in your old bedroom tonight."

"That's wonderful!" Emil looked delighted at the news.

Colby looked questionable. "They all canceled?"

"Yeah, something about a soccer game," Sadie lied easily, Remy noticed. This wasn't the first time Sadie had lied to Colby. And by the way he was looking at her, he wasn't buying it.

When Sadie went out back with Emil, he turned to Remy.

"That's really nice of you, but I have to admit, I'm a little bummed out."

"That I'm having a sleepover?" she asked, then she thought about it. She didn't even ask if that would be okay. "I'm sorry. I should have run it by you first."

"No, that's not why." Colby shook his head. "I wanted to invite you out to dinner tonight."

She froze. "Oh."

Colby shrugged. "I guess I'll have to wait for another night."

"I'm not doing anything tomorrow," she threw out, hoping he would want to reschedule. "I heard there's this really neat farm-to-table restaurant in Bar Harbor."

"Would you like to go to dinner with me?" he asked.

Remy couldn't hide her smile. "I would love to."

"Great, I'll get a reservation and let you know when I bring Sadie over for her sleepover." He backed away from the counter. "The sleepover is really nice of you."

"Of course," she said, then she added, "I look forward to dinner."

"I do too," he said.

And she wondered if he could hear her heart thumping wildly. "I'll see you later."

She bit her bottom lip, thinking about what might become of tomorrow night.

Colby backed into the office door and disappeared. Remy didn't know what to think or if she should even think about what had just happened. She should just take in the moment. Things were good. She didn't need to worry about the next moment or if the good would fall apart. All she needed to think about was that she wanted to make a young teenager's night and had a date with a very attractive lobsterman.

Things were good.

And just when she was about to put her phone away, Roland walked through the doors.

"Hi, Roland," she said, suddenly feeling uncomfortable

meeting him here. Should she tell him about her date with Colby? Should she tell Colby about Roland? Did she not say anything to anyone and figure she was an adult who could do what she wanted? "How are you?"

"I'm good," he said, looking around. "Looking for some lobster for dinner tonight."

"Sounds good," she said.

"Would you be free?" he asked.

"Oh, I wish I was, but unfortunately, I have a sleepover," she said with a little giggle. She was about to go into the story when she noticed his face pucker up.

"You have a sleepover?" he asked.

"Yes, with Sadie," she said. She had mentioned Sadie to him before. "The young girl who's always in the market."

"Why?" The sour look twisted his face even further.

"Because her friends ditched her and—" She stopped herself from explaining. "Did you want those lobsters?"

Roland shrugged. "I thought we were going to have dinner."

"You never said tonight," she reminded him. "I'm sorry if there was a miscommunication."

"How about tomorrow?" he asked. "We could have dinner and see a movie."

"I thought you wanted to talk about my designs for your space?" She noticed he hadn't brought up the design project.

"If we have dinner, we can talk all about it then," he said.

But as he checked his phone, not noticing a clear change in her demeanor, she realized she didn't want to have dinner with him. And she wasn't sure she wanted to work with someone who gave her ultimatums. That had been Joe's style, and she no longer dealt with that kind of behavior.

"I'll have to check my schedule," she said, but she didn't check her phone sitting on the counter in front of her.

"Sure, let me know," he said, but his body shifted away from her, and his energy changed. "I should be going."

With a quick wave, Roland began to leave the market.

"We can discuss your kitchen ideas," he said as he reached the door.

"Maybe," she said, being even more vague.

She watched Roland get into his car before giving another customer her attention. If she had been with a true design firm, he'd been charged hourly for what she had done, and now it looked like she had done it all for free. Why hadn't she seen that he had no intentions of using her as an interior designer? She was such an idiot.

She left the counter and went out back as soon as her shift was over. Bridgette came in and asked all about the sleepover.

"I think that's a great idea," Bridgette said. "Sadie's been so lost these days."

Remy didn't know why she hadn't thought of this before. "Come over too. Bring the baby and we can all hang out."

"No, no, you should do this with just Sadie," Bridgette said. "She deserves a little bit of girl pampering. Things have been so busy with the baby and me. It's hard having all your attention taken away."

Remy hadn't thought about the baby's arrival and what that might do to a young girl who had already lost her parents.

She and Bridgette walked out together, and Remy kissed Camden on the top of her head, taking in a deep breath before leaving the baby.

She stopped by the grocery store before heading home. She picked up ice cream, sprinkles, chocolate sauce, and cherries. She got popcorn kernels and butter to make homemade popcorn. She picked up chips and other snacks and lots of candy, all different types. She got hot cocoa and sodas. In the morning, she'd make Belgian waffles, hashbrowns and sausage, with orange juice and chocolate milk. Remy would give Sadie a sleepover that she would never forget.

At exactly six on the dot, the pizza arrived just as Sadie and Colby did.

"You ready to have a night of awesomeness?" Remy asked, already in her pajamas.

Sadie, also in her pajamas and slippers, held a stuffed bear. "I'm so ready. I brought tons of cookies Nana made and some games."

"Great!" Remy opened the door and Sadie walked right in, dropping her backpack onto the floor in the front hall.

"Make yourself comfortable, Sadie." Colby stood on the front porch with a sleeping bag and a pillow. "Where would you like these?"

"Oh, is she expecting to sleep on the floor?" Remy had a bed all made up in the attic for her.

"She'll probably fall asleep watching the movie," Colby said. "She hasn't even stayed up past midnight on New Year's Eve."

Remy was relieved to hear that. "I was worried about that. I don't think I'll even make it to midnight myself."

"This is wicked nice of you," Colby said. "She's so excited." He stuffed his hands into his pockets. "Thanks, Remy."

An electric pulse jolted through Remy's body as he looked at her.

If Sadie hadn't interrupted the two of them, and if Remy had been able to speak, she swore something would have happened right then. There was no doubt.

"You ready to do pedis?" Sadie asked, bouncing in from the kitchen.

"Yeah, totally," Remy said, heat crawling up her chest. "Let's do it."

"I'll pick you up in the morning," Colby said to Sadie before kissing her on the cheek.

"Bye, Uncle Colby!" Sadie pushed her uncle out the door— literally—and shut it before he even had a chance to say anything else. "So, where should we do our pedis?"

They started in the family room with their pedis while watching Remy's pick, a classic rom-com called *13 Going on 30*. Then they went to the kitchen to make ice cream sundaes and played Yahtzee. Sadie chose the second movie, *Pitch Perfect*, as Remy made popcorn in the kitchen.

"Go ahead and start it," Remy said as she heated up the oil in a pot, just like Gordon had done for them as kids.

"Okay," Sadie said, pressing play with the remote control, completely at home.

Remy smiled to herself as she looked around. This was the kind of night she had loved with her mom and Meredith. The kind of night where they'd sit around watching movies, talking about everything, and playing games. She never thought it would happen again after her mom had died.

Just as the popcorn started to pop, headlights flashed across the room and startled Remy. She looked out and saw an unfamiliar car shut off, and a woman got out.

"It's Melanie!" Sadie called out.

"Melanie?" Remy said, unsure who Melanie was.

Sadie ran to the door.

"Sadie, don't open up the door to strangers," Remy said, warning her.

"She's not a stranger," Sadie said. "She's my aunt!"

Sadie swung open the door and ran into the woman's arms.

A sinking sensation swept through Remy as she now knew exactly who it was. "Hello. I'm Remy."

The woman stood up and laughed, reaching out her hand. "Melanie." She turned to Sadie, who clapped her hands together, still delighted to see her aunt. "So, it didn't take long for your uncle to replace me now, did it?"

CHAPTER 22

*C*olby didn't even know what to say when he saw Melanie standing in front of his parents' market as he went to lock up for the night.

"I should've called," she said. "I didn't mean to upset anyone."

He stuffed his hands into his pockets—a habit he did to stay still. He wished he could do it inside his head, keep his thoughts still. So many thoughts raced through his head. "What are you doing back?"

"I wanted to see you and maybe talk." Her eyes didn't meet his, which was a telltale sign she had more to say.

"What is it?" he asked right away, not willing to play games. "What do you want?"

"I wanted to try again." This time, she looked him dead in the eyes. "I miss you. I miss us."

He wished he had taken Remy's advice and bought benches for the front of the market. He needed to take a seat. "You want to try again?"

She clasped her hands together. "I know I don't deserve your sympathy, but I've missed you. My day is empty without you. I just want to talk to you and hold you and smell you."

She stepped closer to him, but he took a step back. "It's been two years."

"I broke our marriage," she said. "I know that's unforgivable, but we had been together since high school. I had never been on my own. I just wanted to see if there was something I was missing. And it was you. It was only you."

"You left when Sadie came to stay with us," he reminded her. "I needed your help and you left."

He didn't want to remind her of their darkest moment, but there it was. He couldn't get past that. She may have left the marriage, but he could never forgive her for what she had said about his family that night.

"I'm sorry for all the things I said," she said. "But Brynn was reckless with that little girl."

Colby clenched his jaw, holding back all the things he wanted to say. He didn't want to do this anymore. The fighting, the anxiety, the what-ifs. Melanie had been a big part of his life, and he didn't want to be that to be tainted by making things even worse. He just started to move on again with his life.

"I'm sorry too, but I can't go back," he said. "I loved you most of my life, and I've missed you too, but I'm not in love with you anymore. And honestly, I don't think you are either."

"I do love you, Colby," she pleaded. "I thought what I was doing was the right thing at the time. She had a problem."

Colby didn't say anything. What more was there to say? He didn't move from his spot. He didn't want her to leave or to stay. He didn't want any of this. Why did she have to come back into town? Why did she have to stir things up? Because now everything was murky. He couldn't see straight.

"Who is she?" Melanie asked.

"Who is who?" he said, but he knew she was referring to Remy. He had received a text from Sadie telling him she visited the house. "She's a very good friend."

"Right." Melanie pressed her palms together. "I see."

They stood silent for a moment. He couldn't even hear the waves.

"Does she make you happy?" Melanie asked.

"She does," he said, keeping his hands inside his pockets.

Melanie walked up to him and gave him a hug. "I wish nothing but the best for you Colby."

And Melanie walked away.

He didn't stop her or even offer a goodbye. This was her hometown too, but she seemed more like a stranger than a resident.

"Melanie," he called out after her.

She stopped and turned around, facing him.

He didn't move from where he stood. "Good luck with everything. I hope you find what you're looking for."

Melanie didn't reply. Instead, she just turned and left without saying anything.

And suddenly, all the weight of the divorce, the anger and pain, floated off his back, and he instantly felt lighter.

He walked back into the store, not knowing what to do. If Melanie had stopped by the store, then she would have stopped by the house.

He grabbed his keys.

When he pulled up, he could see the television flashing colors throughout a dark room. He looked at the time: ten.

He decided to text the both of them.

You up? he texted them.

Sadie answered first. **Of course! It's a sleepover.**

Yup, Remy texted back.

He reread the one word over and over. What did that mean? Was she up and upset having had to deal with meeting Melanie tonight?

Lucy would say he was lovesick over Melanie when they had first started dating. When he hadn't been around her, he'd mope around and be down in the dumps.

That was what he felt now when he wasn't around Remy. He

wanted to be around her all the time. He spent his days thinking about her, his nights wanting to see her. She consumed all his thoughts.

He texted back. **Can I stop in?**

Sadie texted back. **Girls only.**

Remy didn't text, but he noticed the curtain pull back, and she gave him a little wave.

Soon the back door opened, and Remy peeked her head out. "Want to come in for some hot cocoa?"

"I'd love some," he said, not sure what his plan was. He followed her inside, craning his neck to see Sadie lying on the floor in front of the television, her hands free of any devices. "No phone?"

"We agreed to put them on the coffee table and only respond to family texts," Remy said, lifting her chin to Sadie. "It was her idea."

Colby was impressed. Sadie couldn't go anywhere without her beloved phone. "It was the worst thing I ever got her."

Remy shrugged. "I don't know. It's how it's modeled, you know?"

"Remy," he said, getting right to the heart of his visit. "My ex-wife and I have a very long past and—"

"You don't have to explain anything," she said, putting the kettle on the stove, facing her back to him. "It's none of my business."

He held the back of a chair at the kitchen table. If she didn't think it was her business, did he feel something she didn't?

"I was kind of hoping you'd want to know," he said, waiting for her reaction. But she didn't move.

"Why's that?" Remy spooned out the cocoa and plopped it into a mug. Then she turned around holding the ceramic cup with both hands.

His eyes held onto hers as his heart thudded against his ribs. "Because I hoped you'd want to know my situation."

She blinked quickly. "Your situation?"

He nodded, taking a deep breath. This was the moment. He could no longer hide from the truth. Either she felt something or she didn't, but either way, he needed to get his feelings off his chest.

"I wanted you to know that there's nothing between my ex-wife and I." He squeezed the wood, keeping his eyes on her.

"Okay," she said, not moving from the stove, still holding the mug.

"Melanie and I had much bigger problems than anyone in this small town knows," he said, wondering what she had heard about the relationship.

"Oh," she said.

Her one syllable responses were starting to freak him out. "I just wanted you to know in case you might have heard otherwise or—"

The kettle began to steam, and the whistle screamed out. Remy quickly removed it from the burner and set it on a cool one. She turned back around, holding the mug. He hoped nothing had changed since dropping off Sadie that evening.

"Where shall we go for dinner?" she asked.

His heart immediately slowed down in relief, and he let out a laugh. "A place called Luca's."

"That sounds fabulous," she said, picking up the kettle and pouring him a mug of cocoa. "We're finishing up Sadie's movie now, but we were going to play a game of Monopoly if you want to join us."

"It's a girls only sleepover!" Sadie called from the living room.

They both laughed at this, and she handed him his cocoa.

He took a drink from the mug. "This is good."

She smiled. "Those Swiss really know how to make a good hot chocolate."

"In the winter, we should do some of this in a hot cocoa basket," he suggested, taking another drink.

She made a face. "You need my help more than I thought."

"I do," he admitted, looking into her blue eyes, hoping she believed him.

He had so much to say, but had no words to really express how he felt.

"I thought I didn't need anyone in my life." He stopped, feeling more like a fool with each passing second. But he needed to express his feelings before it was too late. "I can't stop thinking about you or wanting to talk to you or hear from you. Ever since you came into my life, things have made sense. Life suddenly makes sense. You opened my eyes to new possibilities and ways of thinking. I realize now that I need you, Remy."

She didn't say anything, and he heard the volume on the television turn down.

"Colby," she said, her fingers playing with the edge of the table. "There are things I want in my life, and I don't want to compromise my wants anymore—for anyone."

"I'd never ask you to." He didn't know what she wanted for her life, but he wanted to be there along the way. "I just want to help you get whatever it is you want."

He reached out his hand and placed it on hers. Then he heard a heavy breath release from her chest.

"I'm sorry, Colby, but I want more than what you can give me."

CHAPTER 23

*R*emy pulled back her hand, expecting Colby to react, but not sure how he would.

His forehead creased. After an agonizing silence, he said, "Okay, then. I should probably head out and leave you girls to your sleepover."

Remy bit her bottom lip, wishing she was better with words, but her structure was backwards, and her message came out wrong.

"Colby, wait," she said as he set his cocoa down. "I want to apply to be a foster parent."

Remy waited for what he had to say, but he said nothing.

So, she decided to start at the beginning.

"I didn't want to take the job at the market," she said, confessing the truth. "But these past few weeks have been the happiest I've had in a really long time. This little village has become more of a home than any place I've lived before. And I want to make this place a home for a child who needs a mom," she said, tears instantly stinging the backs of her eyes. "I want to become a foster mom, and I don't want to compromise on that."

She had come so far, yet she had a lot further to go, and she didn't want anything to get in her way.

"I totally understand if that's too much," she quickly threw out. "But I've wanted this for a really long time now, and I'm not willing to give that dream up again."

Remy looked away, feeling drained by her truth. Maybe she wasn't a very maternal person. Maybe she was just an auntie kind of person who had sleepovers every once in a while.

But instead of running away, Colby stepped closer to her.

"How can I help?" he asked.

Remy looked up from her hands. He was so close she could smell his sandalwood scent. "Just support me."

That was all she needed. Support. She didn't need someone to tell her what to do. She didn't need someone's money. She didn't need someone to make promises. She just wanted support to do what she wanted.

"You'll have to get a bedroom ready," he said, squeezing her hand. "We could talk about it over dinner."

She smiled. "I'd love that."

She noticed the volume to the television went back up.

Colby stretched his neck, glancing into the living room, then he took Remy's hand and pulled her toward the door.

"Night, Sadie!" he said, opening the back door and stepping out, still pulling Remy along with him.

"Night, Uncle Colby!" she said from the living room, the volume going up even more.

Colby pulled Remy onto the front porch and closed the door behind them, then he took her hands into his. He shifted closer to her, and she could feel the heat from his body against hers, charging every cell in her body. Then slowly, he lightly brushed the back of his fingers against her cheek, pushing loose strands of hair away from her face. His breath tickled her lips, and she closed her eyes as he led her to his kiss.

Electric jolts shot through her body as he wrapped his arms around her waist, and she kissed him back under the moonlight. The world around them seemed to disappear as he embraced her.

Out of breath, they separated, their chests expanding together in rhythm. She could feel he wanted to kiss her more.

"I should watch the ending of the movie," she said, out of breath.

He nodded but kissed her again, pulling her into him, pressing his body against hers.

Then just as quickly, Colby ran down the porch steps to his truck. "I'll be back tomorrow to pick Sadie and you up for the day."

"The day?" she asked.

"We have a date," he said, but he didn't share any more information.

"I have a shift at the market tomorrow."

"Consider this on-the-job training." He got into his truck and pulled out.

Remy stood on the porch, watching Colby drive away. Warmth spread throughout her body, even though the night air was chilly.

She smiled to herself as she walked back into the house.

"Ooooo...I saw someone kissing..." Sadie teased.

Remy couldn't control her blushing, even at the teasing of a thirteen-year-old.

"Do you want to hear the tea?" Remy said, laughing at herself.

She told Sadie some of the details, like how she had a crush on her uncle, and that he was a good kisser. She kept the other stuff private, like how she was certain she was falling in love with him.

"You know," Sadie said as the movie finished, "you'll need someone to help if you get a foster kid. Like a babysitter."

Sadie didn't look at Remy as she said this, but Remy could feel her vulnerability as she waited for Remy's response.

"I was hoping you'd help me." Remy moved closer to where Sadie sat and put her arm around her shoulder. "I need all the help I can get, like figuring out what kinds of dinners kids like and going to sports events and all the stuff that comes with being a mom."

"You'll need a better car," Sadie said.

"What's wrong with my car?" Remy didn't think she would have to get a bigger car for now.

"It's like, all posh. You're going to have baby food and throw up or worse on those leather seats," Sadie said.

This made Remy laugh, and excitement fluttered in her belly like it had when she'd found out she was pregnant.

She was going to be a mom.

CHAPTER 24

$\mathcal{C}$olby showed up exactly at ten o'clock and could smell breakfast sausage wafting out from inside the house.

He could hear laughter and a lot more voices than just Remy's and Sadie's coming from the kitchen.

When he reached the door, he saw Remy's whole family sitting around the kitchen table, with Sadie as the center of attention. He didn't knock, instead watching from afar as Sadie made the group of adults, including Kyle, laugh in hysterics. He only knocked on the door when he heard his niece say his name.

"It's Uncle Colby!" Sadie said, pointing at him through the door's window.

This made the rest of them laugh. What kinds of stories had Sadie been telling them?

"Hi, Colby," Remy said, opening the door. "Good morning."

She leaned over and kissed him on the cheek, and he spoke into her ear.

"You look beautiful." He said it without thinking about the others sitting in the room and wasn't sure if that made her uncomfortable or not. He handed her a bouquet of flowers. "For you."

"Thank you," she said, putting the flowers up to her nose and inhaling their sweet scent. "They're gorgeous." She looked down and noticed the basket he held. "Is that another basket?'

"You've really rubbed off on me." He handed it over to her. "I think you'll like this one. Or at least appreciate it. You'll probably have some suggestions, but I think—"

"Uncle Colby, just let her open it," Sadie said from across the room.

This made everyone laugh.

Remy put the basket on the counter and opened the cover. Inside, he had items based on the theme of becoming a foster mother. Bridgette had been a godsend and helped him out. She gave him a mother's journal she had never used, a big fuzzy blanket, a parenting guide for different stages of childhood, along with a book on becoming a foster mother he had picked up at the Department of Health and Human services that morning.

"When did you get this?" She flipped through the pages. "I can't believe it."

"Wow, Colby," Meredith said. "That's really nice."

"Quinn helped me out," Colby said. "He owed me for missing poker night."

Quinn held up his hands. "I just ran down to the county courthouse and talked to someone about the process."

Remy's eyes glistened. "Wow, that's really thoughtful."

She pulled out a small box. For this surprise, he had to put in a huge favor with his buddy Cliff, the owner of Blueberry Bay's only jewelry store.

"Colby," she said, holding the cardboard jewelry box. "You shouldn't have."

"Open it," he said. He shot a look at Sadie, hoping she saw what he got.

Remy pulled the cover off and gasped. "A mermaid charm!"

She pulled the charm out of the box.

"I love it," she said, removing her bracelet from her wrist.

Sadie jumped off her chair and ran to Remy, helping her open the bracelet. "You have to twist this part to get it to come apart."

Sadie held up her charm bracelet. "It's the same charm as mine!"

Remy grabbed hold of Sadie and pulled her into a big hug. "We're mermaid sisters."

Colby ended up joining the group at the table, and they sat for a couple hours talking and telling stories of Blueberry Bay and their lives in Andover. He sat next to Remy and across from Sadie, who carried along in the conversation the whole time, forgetting her phone in the other room.

He hadn't seen Sadie that happy in a long time.

He hadn't felt that happy in a real long time.

When Remy's family left the three of them cleaned up the kitchen together. Colby worked on the dishes while Remy and Sadie put the food and clean dishes away. By the time they were finished, Sadie had found her phone in the living room and left Colby and Remy alone in the kitchen.

"What do you want to do today?" she asked.

"Well, I thought we could go buy some paint," he suggested. "Then take a boat ride while we plan out how you want to decorate the house."

"I'd really like that," she said, playing with his fingers. "And what about you? What can I do to help you?"

"You already have." He didn't have enough patience to sit there and go through the list of things she had done to help him, Instead, he leaned against the table, pulling her toward him, and nestled her in his arms. He took his fingertips and glided her chin toward him, then softly kissed her on the lips. "You have no idea how much you've helped me see how happy I can be in my life."

That was what Remy had done for him that no one else ever had. She'd shown him the things he already had that made him happy. His family. His niece. His work. His family's traditions. The market.

"What if you became manager?" he said suddenly. "You could run the store, and I could get back out on the water and supply the lobster."

He didn't need to be there. She could run that place better than all the St. Germains combined.

"Unless you don't want to," he said, wishing he had planned that out better. Being a manager at a dinky market was probably the last thing Remy wanted to do.

"I can't take your job," she said, shaking her head.

"Managing the market isn't what I want to be doing. I want to be fishing for lobsters." he said, holding her hand. "There would be a big pay increase."

"Only if you need my help," she said, squeezing it.

He squeezed back. "I really do need your help."

She looked at him, her beauty so real and raw and ravishing, it took everything in his body not to kiss her again.

"I'd love to," she said.

And he kissed her—hard at first, tasting her, holding her against his body. But he soon slowed his kissing, taking in her sweet scent, and looked at her.

"Did I ever tell you how glad I am that you parked in my spot that day?" he said, holding her chin with his palm.

This made her laugh, and an electric energy shot through his whole body.

She kissed him again, pulling out his lip with hers. "Do I get to park there now?"

He shrugged. "It's up to the manager."

Remy threw her arms around his neck and kissed him again, a long, lingering kiss that made his toes curl.

As they parted, she whispered in his ear. "Let's start painting Emil's old bedroom."

CHAPTER 25

*A*fter a long spring, summer had finally arrived in the little village of Blueberry Bay, and the town was getting ready for the big Lobster Festival, which the Queen Bees decided to host this year. Colby was certain the Queen's newest member, Remy, had something to do with it, but she wouldn't admit it. Somehow, she always knew how to get people excited about going to the market and buying lobster. It was her gift, which worked out great for him because he was the one catching it.

Over the past few months, Remy had taken over as manager, and the Harbor Market was thriving. She got people to come in and buy the fish along with other specialty items one could only find in Blueberry Bay.

He pulled up to the docks after dropping Remy off at the market and stopped dead in his tracks when he saw Brynn standing next to his fishing boat.

"Hi, fishbrains," she said. His sister had been his little sister but also his best friend his whole life. Just hearing her voice again made his heart ache because he knew it wasn't going to last. She'd take off like all the other times and break his family's hearts once again.

"What are you doing here?" he asked, not sure what this visit meant. Was she out of money? Was she in trouble? Had she fallen for some rotten guy again?

"Sadie called me." Brynn shook her head and rubbed her hands together. The spring morning wasn't that cool compared to others, but he suspected his sister was nervous to say what she had come to say.

"And?" He wanted this over with.

"She says she met a woman who takes good care of her." Brynn choked out the last part, and he could tell this news had been painful.

"She's referring to my girlfriend," he said, hoping this wouldn't break his sister. "Her name is Remy, and she's great with Sadie."

Brynn looked away, wiping her face with her sleeve. "She says she's nice and stuff."

Colby nodded, noticing Brynn's familiar addiction twitch. "She is."

"So, she's still good with you?" Brynn asked Colby. She scratched her shoulder. Then her neck. Then her arm.

He nodded again, keeping his voice level and calm. He wasn't frightened about what Brynn might do to him but what she might do to herself.

"You're better for her anyway," Brynn said quickly.

"No, she'd be better with her mother," Colby replied.

Brynn pulled out a cigarette and lit it immediately, then took a long drag. She shook her head as she blew out. "Now I know you're lying."

"She loves you, and so do we," he said, wishing he could grab hold of her, take her home with him, and get her better. "We want you to come back home." He could still see his baby sister in her eyes. "But you have to be clean."

There was no other stipulation. She had to be clean.

She drew in another long drag, the tip of the cigarette blazing orange at its end, and blew out the smoke. He hated the idea that Sadie might go back to her, but the law could grant it if she got clean. But would Brynn ever clean up? And how long before the next relapse? The truth broke his heart because he'd never trust Brynn with Sadie.

"I need you to figure things out," he said, but Brynn was erratic at best, and she wouldn't figure anything out. "She needs her mom."

Tears formed in her eyes. "I just want to be someone she's proud of."

The tears fell down her face.

Colby stayed silent, letting her air her feelings and keeping his own to himself. Because he'd done the lecture, the good cop, the bad cop, the forgiver, all of it. And nothing had ever changed her.

"I just can't do it by myself," she said.

"Then go to rehab," he pushed.

She tapped her cigarette, letting the dirty ash hit the dock. He would've made a comment to anyone else in the world except for Brynn. His sister had always been more fragile than the rest of the world.

"I'm sorry I messed up," she said, sniffling.

"I'm not the one you need to apologize to."

"I just thought I could control it this time," she said, still not agreeing to any of his stipulations.

"I can help, Brynn, but you have to be clean," he said. "We can all help you."

Brynn sobbed in her hands at that point. She had never been able to handle the hard stuff in life. Quitting would be hard. Cleaning up and becoming sober would be hard. Brynn didn't do hard.

He reached out his arms to hug her, but she pushed him back and took a drag of her cigarette. Then she knelt down, dipping the cigarette into the water and putting it out. She held the damp cigarette in her hand, knowing better than to litter in front of Colby.

"I need help," she said.

"I can help."

"No, I need money," she said, the tears gone, the twitch back.

"I have to get out on the water," Colby said. "Come back when you're ready for some real help."

"Colby," she said. "Make sure she knows I love her."

But before he could say anything more, Brynn walked away to an unfamiliar car with an unfamiliar guy inside it.

He watched as the car drove away, wondering when he'd see his sister again. If he'd see her again.

How could he tell his niece her mother loved her when she hadn't even tried to say hello? Did he lie and spare Sadie's feelings?

He didn't go on the boat. Instead, he walked up the docks to the market. Thoughts rolled around in his head. How could Brynn be so selfish? How could she leave without trying to get clean?

"Hey," Remy said, stopping what she was doing as he walked up. She was arranging the tables out front. She had started selling fresh herbs and flowers outside the market. "Did you forget something?"

He walked straight up to her and put his arms around her, holding onto her. "No, I just wanted to see you."

She held him for a long moment, not saying anything. "You sure you're okay?"

He nodded. He was more than okay. He was blessed with what he had. "Brynn came by the docks."

Remy's eyes widened, instantly panicked. "What did she want?"

"She said Sadie told her about you," he said.

"Oh?" Her forehead wrinkled in empathy, but worry still hung in the creases of her face. "And?"

He shrugged. "And she left."

"I'm sorry," she said, looking into his eyes. "It must be so hard to see her unwell."

He had told Remy everything from Brynn's first drink in high school to stealing from neighbors' medicine cabinets to Melanie calling the police on her. Remy knew everything about him, and he knew everything about her.

He kissed her before letting her go.

"I'll see you tonight, then," he said, hoping Sadie would keep mum on the plans.

"I'll see you at the house," she said.

He gave her another kiss and took off toward his boat. He should've been out on the water a half hour ago.

He glanced back one last time, and Remy had gone back to arranging the plants, smiling as she watered them. He smiled to himself. He couldn't wait for tonight.

CHAPTER 26

*R*emy cleaned when she got home. She didn't know what Colby had planned that evening, but by the way he had been acting all day and the way Sadie had been avoiding her, she imagined it was big.

"Knock, knock," she heard Meredith call out from the front door. "I come bearing gifts."

Meredith and Gordon walked into the house, both with baskets in their hands. "Carolyn finished these last night."

There had to have been over a dozen different baskets weaved together from seagrass. "These are beautiful."

"She does it while watching her shows," Gordon said. "Ginny said she's even slowed down on the drinking."

"Really? Who would've thought basket weaving would make Carolyn stop with the cocktails?"

"Here," Gordon said, handing over a stack of envelopes. "I picked up your mail."

On the top of the pile, Remy saw the state's DMV return address. "I got my new license!"

She ripped open the envelope and pulled out the plastic license.

"That's a great picture," Gordon said, typical of her father, who couldn't even see up close.

But Remy looked down at her image and had to agree. That had been her best picture yet.

"You look really happy," Meredith said, checking out the photo.

Remy nodded in agreement. "I am."

She pulled out her old license, the one that had her married name, and grabbed a pair of scissors, cutting it in half and throwing it into the trash. She picked up the new license, the one that read Remy Jacqueline Johnson, along with her new address, and put it into her wallet.

"Why don't we have Sunday dinner here tomorrow?" Remy suggested. "I can cook everything and we can have dinner on the porch."

"Are you sure?" Meredith asked, but Remy could tell her sister didn't mind at all. "That sounds great."

"We'll have a lobster bake," Remy said. "Colby went out this morning to drop some pots. I'm sure we can get enough for all of us."

From the living room, Remy heard her phone start to ring. She ran toward the sound and grabbed it without even looking at the number.

"Hello?" she said into the phone.

"Yes, hello. I'm calling to speak to Ms. Remy Johnson," a woman's voice said on the other line.

"This is Remy Johnson," she said.

"Hello, Ms. Johnson. My name is Barbara Wood," the woman said. "I'm the social worker you met from the state department."

Remy had to catch her breath. She covered the mouthpiece and said to the group, "It's the social worker!" She could barely get the words out. "Yes, hello, Ms. Wood. I remember meeting with you."

"Would you be ready to take in a child as soon as this

evening?" the woman said. "We have a three-year-old boy who is in need of a placement as soon as possible."

"There's a child who needs to come here tonight?" she asked, unsure if she understood the circumstances. The whole room quieted down after she said that.

"A three-year-old named Matthew," the social worker said.

Tears sprung to Remy's eyes. She looked up and knew her mother was there, and she knew her baby Matthew was there, too. There may not be mermaids in the sea, but there were angels up in heaven.

Remy let out a laugh at the coincidence. Her Matthew would have been three.

Meredith and Gordon moved to the doorway, listening in. She gave a nod to them. Meredith covered her mouth with one of her hands as Gordon squeezed her shoulder from behind.

"I'll have a room ready," she said, her heart pounding in her chest.

"He should arrive later this afternoon," the woman said. "He'll have a few items but will need some more."

"Yes, of course," Remy said. "I'll get whatever he needs."

"Great," the woman said. "I'll let you know when we're close."

"Perfect. Thank you so much." Remy couldn't believe this day was actually happening. All this time, waiting for this moment.

"So?" Meredith said as soon as Remy hung up.

Remy held the phone against her chest. "I'm going to be a foster mom!"

Meredith rushed to Remy and gave her a huge hug. Gordon clapped his hands and put his arms around both of his daughters.

"I'm going to be an auntie!" Meredith said.

"I'm going to be a grandpop again," Gordon said, a look of pride across his face.

"Will you tell Ginny and the Queens?" Remy would get all the help she could. "I need some sweet treats."

Remy texted Colby right away but knew he wouldn't get the message until he returned to shore. In the meantime, she cleaned and prepared. Meredith ran to the store to get the things Remy still needed in the house, like childproofing stuff and kid-friendly foods.

She texted Sadie after the last bell, and it took the thirteen-year-old twenty minutes to arrive from school.

"It's a boy?" Sadie asked as soon as she walked through the door, dropping her backpack onto the bench where she did every day after school.

Sadie had been the most supportive of Remy's decision to foster a child. Colby said it was because of her own situation, being taken from her mother, but Remy knew that was just part of it.

Sadie had a big heart. She had been great with Camden and had started being a good friend with the young girls in Remy's neighborhood. Remy saw a young lady who wanted to be kind and open her heart to others.

"He's three," Remy said, putting a nightlight in the bathroom.

Sadie went to her backpack and opened it up. "Here."

She handed Remy a stuffed bear.

"What's this?" Remy asked, holding the teddy. She recognized it from the sleepover. "Isn't this yours?"

"My mom gave this to me when she left," Sadie said. "She said it would be there for me when she couldn't be. I think Matthew should have it because I don't need it anymore."

Remy's heart melted at the gesture. "I think that's a very sweet thing to do. Why don't we put it on his bed."

When Colby arrived, the whole house was filled with Remy's family, Sadie, and the all the Queen Bees dropping off baked goods and other items.

"Hey," he said, walking through the crowd.

"Hey," Remy said back to him. "Did you get my message?"

"I did," he said, still in his fisherman gear. "I came as soon as I could."

She laughed at his orange Grundéns. "I guess so."

"When's he getting here?" he asked.

"Any minute now," she said, looking at her phone. "The social worker said she'd text before he got here."

Ginny got up from the couch. "We should get going and not frighten the poor boy with all us old folks."

Gordon nodded, patting Colby on the back. "Let us know when it's a good time for an introduction."

Remy nodded, then hugged Gordon. "I will."

Meredith hugged Remy as well, while also giving Colby a wink. "We'll see you all later. Let us know how everything goes when you have a chance."

The Queens also began to leave.

"Do I have to go?" Sadie asked.

Remy shook her head. "No, I want you to be one of the first people he meets."

Sadie lifted her shoulders as though she felt important.

"I want you to be here for this, too," Colby said.

Remy noticed a light gleam on his forehead. Was he sweating?

"Remy?" he said, facing her.

"Are you okay?" she asked, noticing his face flushing.

"I am. I've never been better actually." That's when he got down on one knee and said, "Remy Johnson, I want to start being a family, today. Will you marry me?"

"She'll say yes!" Sadie cried out, and it made Remy laugh out loud.

He held out a ring to her. A perfect diamond ring.

"When did you get this?" she asked. They had talked casually about maybe moving in together and getting engaged down the road, but they had only been dating a few months.

"I want Matthew and Sadie and us to all be a family," Colby said. "I want to live here and wake up beside you. I want to sit on the porch and watch the sunset next to you. And I want to start that family now." He looked up at her. "So? What do you think?"

"Yes, I would love to marry you." She got down on her knees and kissed him, wrapping her arms around him. "Yes. Yes. Yes."

They kissed for a long time, laughing at the fact he was in his

Grundéns while he proposed, and Sadie kept yelling, "Put a ring on it!"

Colby then put the ring on her finger and kissed her again. "I love you."

"I love you, too," she said, holding his face with her hands, not willing to let go just yet.

A ding went off on Remy's phone, and Sadie rushed to the coffee table to grab it. "It's them! They're here!"

Colby and Remy stood up together, holding each other's hand.

"You ready to do this?" Colby asked Remy.

She looked out the window at the car parked in the driveway. She could see a little boy's face in the window. "I've never been more ready."

She took Colby's hand, and they walked out the front door with Sadie.

Remy then turned to her and said, "You ready to meet your new little brother?"

CHAPTER 27

*R*emy stretched out her arm as far as she could to reach the edge of the mural with the tip of her paintbrush. She had worked all morning and still hadn't even finished the clouds.

"Lindy, I'm going to take forever," she said to her former boss, who stood underneath making sure Remy didn't fall and break her neck.

"I know," Lindy said. "But that's okay. Besides, we miss you around here, so take all the time you need."

Remy smiled at that. "Thanks, Lindy."

She owed a debt of gratitude to the diner's owner. Lindy had taken her in with no work experience and no recommendations, when she could've easily shown her the door.

"I think they're wonderful clouds," Victor, a regular, said.

She stepped down off the ladder and took another look from far away. Maybe she should lighten the clouds a little more?

"There's mom," a familiar voice said from behind.

Remy swung around to see Sadie standing at the front door holding Matthew's hand.

"Hi, guys!" Remy turned to the little boy. "What's going on?"

"He wanted to have Lindy's waffles," Sadie said. "But I told him we can't eat here this morning. We're just picking you up."

Remy looked at Lindy, feeling guilty for not explaining why they weren't having her famous waffles at the diner. "We're having everyone over for Grandpop's birthday lunch."

"I'll forgive you this time," Lindy teased. "Tell the old buzzard happy birthday from all of us."

"I will," Remy said, wiping her hands clean with a towel. "Let me just clean up and we can go home and get ready for everyone to come over."

Remy put her stuff down as Matthew tugged on her pant leg. "I'm hungry."

"I know, but we're eating at home," she said to the redheaded, blue-eyed boy.

"How about muffins for the kids while you clean up?" Lindy offered.

"That's very nice of you, Lindy," Remy said, putting the brushes away. "What do you say, kids?"

"Thank you," they said in unison, taking a seat at the counter next to the old gentleman who grumbled about the summer crowds.

"Where's your dad?" Remy asked Matthew, looking out the window. "Is he still at the market?"

That was when she saw Colby walking into the diner. At one point, she might not have noticed the tall lumberjack who wore his signature flannel and baseball cap, but now she thought he was the most handsome man she'd ever seen. He didn't have a fancy title or carry a card with his information on it, but he had a heart of gold and he loved her with all his soul.

"Hey," he said, kissing her as soon as he came close enough. "I was just checking on the new girl."

"She's perfect," Remy said, playfully hitting him on the arm. "Besides, she's my niece. I told you she'd be a great hire."

"Muriel is doing great," Colby agreed. "I just worry Emil will talk her ear off."

"She's having a blast talking to the locals." Remy wasn't worried about it. Her niece didn't complain. Muriel, being a teacher, had the whole summer off and came to stay in Maine. No one mentioned the fact that she hadn't come with her long-term boyfriend, but Muriel would share when she was ready. Remy understood needing time to think through things.

Colby looked at the start of her mural. "It looks great."

She closed up her paints and put her hands on her hips. "It's coming along."

"Well, I think it's a great start," Colby said, and as cheesy as he was being, she appreciated him as her biggest supporter. "Where are you going to put the mermaid?"

She tilted her head at the mural, examining it. "In the corner by the window."

She'd use the mermaid Jacob had painted as inspiration, but with her own take. A young girl as the mermaid, a new generation.

She kissed him again.

"Look at those two," Lindy said to Sadie and Matthew, who were sitting together at the counter. "Do they do this at home too?"

Sadie rolled her eyes at Lindy and nodded. "All the time."

Remy shook her head, but Colby kissed her again.

"Eww," Sadie said.

"Eww," Matthew mimicked.

Remy laughed at the two. She didn't even know what she was laughing at, just that she was incredibly happy. Pure happiness ran all the way through her body down to her toes.

"Just one more week," Colby said to her.

"One more week," she said, thinking about all she needed to do before they officially got married.

Colby had suggested town hall the day Matthew came, but Meredith insisted they wait and use the barn. Sadie would be her flower girl, Meredith her maid of honor, and Matthew would be Colby's best man. They invited only their families and closest friends, but their list included almost everyone in Blueberry Bay. It may be cramped, but it was perfect for Remy. She wanted nothing more than to be Mrs. Colby St. Germain.

"You all done?" she asked Matthew, who had muffin crumbles all over his face.

"Mm-hmm," Matthew said, taking Remy's hand like it had always fit there perfectly and jumped down.

"You want to ask Sadie to grab your teddy?"

"Sadie, will you grab Mr. Bear?" he asked with a slight lisp.

"Sure thing." Sadie picked up Mr. Bear from the chair.

"You guys ready?" Remy asked.

"Yeah!" Matthew said, holding up his free hand, which Colby took in his.

When they got outside, Matthew started begging right away. "Swing me! Swing me!"

He jumped up as soon as Remy and Colby held onto Matthew's hands and they swung him up into the air, lifting his little feet off the ground.

"Higher! Higher!" he cried out as they walked across the parking lot to the minivan.

Sadie opened the side door and got right in, putting her earbuds into her ears.

"Do you guys mind if I have Leah and Jenna over for a sleep-over tomorrow night?" she asked them.

Remy shot a look at Colby, who put Matthew into his car seat. "Sure. That sounds great."

"Do you think we could watch that movie we watched at our sleepover?" Sadie asked Remy.

"You mean *13 Going on 30*?" Remy asked. "Of course. It's an essential for all sleepovers."

Sadie seemed to agree, because she no longer paid any attention to Remy or Colby, who sat in the front seats.

"You ready to go home?" Colby asked her, grabbing her hand over the console.

She looked at him, then back at Matthew, who sang the ABCs,

and then to Sadie, who joined in singing the ABCs with him. Remy squeezed Colby's hand, and the expression he had on his face said he understood what she couldn't say in that moment without getting emotional.

She was ready for this new journey. She was ready to go on this crazy adventure because she had Colby and everyone else by her side. She had the love of this man and her family.

"Ready."

I hope you enjoyed *The Market on Blueberry Bay!* The next book in the series, *The Lighthouse on Blueberry Bay*, focuses on Muriel's journey. Click HERE to see the Blueberry Bay series or check out my other beach romance series HERE!

If you'd like to receive a FREE standalone novella from my Camden Cove series, please click HERE or visit my website at ellenjoyauthor.com.

ALSO BY ELLEN JOY

Click HERE for more information about other books by Ellen Joy.

Feeling Blessed in the Valley

<u>Blueberry Bay</u>
The Cottage on Blueberry Bay
The Market on Blueberry Bay
The Lighthouse on Blueberry Bay
The Fabric Shop on Blueberry Bay

Beach Rose Secrets

ABOUT THE AUTHOR

Ellen lives in a small town in New England, between the Atlantic Ocean and the White Mountains. She lives with her husband, two sons, and one very spoiled puppy princess.

Ellen writes in the early morning hours before her family wakes up. When she's not writing, you can find her spending time with her family, gardening, or headed to the beach. She loves summer and flip-flops, running on a dirt country road, and a sweet love song.

All of her stories are clean romances where families are close, neighbors are nosy, and the couples are destined for each other.

Made in the USA
Monee, IL
11 October 2024

67473918R00134